Angel and Dragon

OTHER BOOKS BY MERIOL TREVOR

The Rose Round
Sun Slower, Sun Faster
The Sparrow Child
Lights in a Dark Town
Shadows and Images

THE LETZENSTEIN CHRONICLES
The Crystal Snowstorm
Following the Phoenix

Angel & Dragon

by
Meriol Trevor

*Letzenstein Chronicles
Book III*

BETHLEHEM BOOKS · IGNATIUS PRESS
WARSAW, N.D.   SAN FRANCISCO

© 1999, Meriol Trevor. All rights reserved.

ISBN 1-883937-27-2
Library of Congress: 98-73484

First printing, May 1999

Cover and interior art © 1999, Mary Beth Owens
Cover design by Davin Carlson

Bethlehem Books • Ignatius Press
15605 County Road 15
Minto, ND 58261
www.bethlehembooks.com

Printed in the United States of America on acid free paper

*To Peter Sharpe
and the young people of Bethlehem Community
in North Dakota, U.S.A.*

Table of Contents

1. Encounter in Trier: 1849 — 1
2. Some Kind of Incident — 17
3. Princes and Peasants — 33
4. Image of Conflict — 47
5. Actual Conflict — 65
6. Trials and Ceremonies — 82
7. Fair at Xandeln — 103
8. Darkness in Summer — 120
9. Two Escapes — 139
10. No Escape — 160
11. Storms Threatening — 178
12. The Last Day — 196

Family Tree of the Grand Dukes of Letzenstein

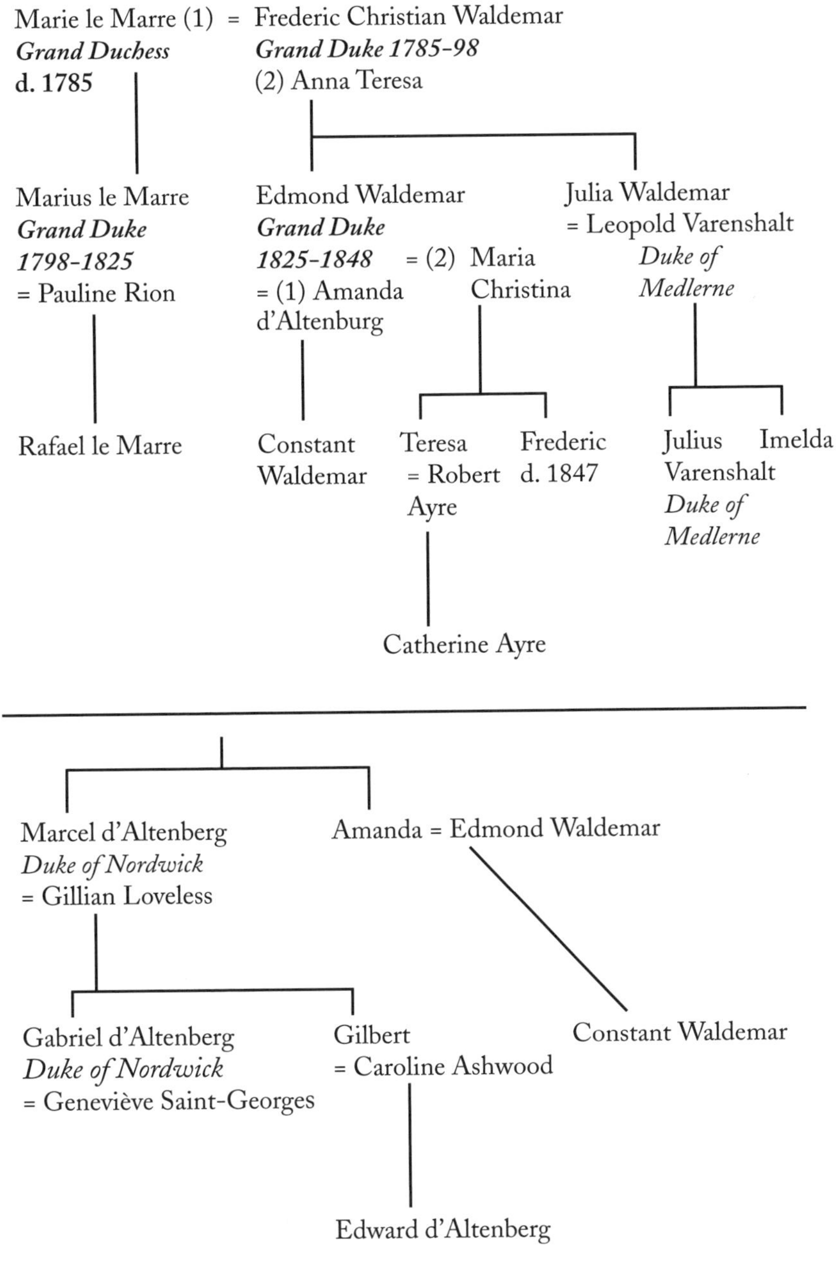

Marie le Marre (1) = Frederic Christian Waldemar
Grand Duchess   *Grand Duke 1785-98*
d. 1785   (2) Anna Teresa

Marius le Marre — *Grand Duke 1798-1825* = Pauline Rion

Edmond Waldemar — *Grand Duke 1825-1848* = (1) Amanda d'Altenburg = (2) Maria Christina

Julia Waldemar = Leopold Varenshalt *Duke of Medlerne*

Rafael le Marre

Constant Waldemar

Teresa = Robert Ayre

Frederic d. 1847

Julius Varenshalt *Duke of Medlerne*

Imelda

Catherine Ayre

Marcel d'Altenberg *Duke of Nordwick* = Gillian Loveless

Amanda = Edmond Waldemar

Gabriel d'Altenberg *Duke of Nordwick* = Geneviève Saint-Georges

Gilbert = Caroline Ashwood

Constant Waldemar

Edward d'Altenberg

1

Encounter in Trier: 1849

GILES AND CATHERINE sat at one of the little tables outside a café in Trier, drinking lemonade. Afternoon was drawing towards evening but the August sun was still warm and after hours spent looking at old churches and ancient Roman walls they were quite glad to sit still and wait for Giles's father to return from calling on a friend. Giles Hawthorne and Catherine Ayre were cousins and they were both fourteen, but they did not know each other well.

Sir Walter Hawthorne, having spent some time in Brussels on a diplomatic mission, was now taking a holiday, travelling first to Aachen and Cologne on the Rhine and then visiting Trier, which was on the Moselle.

"I like Trèves," said Giles, giving the town its French name. "It makes Caesar come alive to think that this was where the Treveri tribe lived, when he was conquering Gaul."

"I like it too," said Catherine, "but I wish we could go on to Letzenstein soon."

Letzenstein, a small independent state between France and Germany, was just across the river, westward.

"Nothing historically important has ever happened in Letzenstein," said Giles. "I can't think why you are so keen on it, considering that last year you seem to have spent most of your time running away from revolutionaries."

Catherine, who looked so quiet and shy, happened to be the daughter of a princess of Letzenstein who had made a runaway marriage with an English officer. She could not remember her parents, who had died in India, leaving her to the care of an old great-aunt in Kent. Until she was thirteen she had not been in her mother's country, but then she had been summoned by her formidable grandfather, the old Grand Duke Edmond Waldemar, and had found herself a pawn in the political power game there.

"It's not just the place, it's the people I like," she said. "My uncle Constant and his cousins—except Julius. I didn't like him at all."

Giles had heard how the Grand Duke had disinherited his son Constant and had tried to make his nephew Julius Varenshalt the Regent for Catherine, on his deathbed. In spite of this, Constant had succeeded to the title, to the satisfaction of the people and to Catherine's relief.

Because Catherine said she did not like Julius, Giles instantly decided that he was probably the only sensible member of Catherine's foreign family.

"I daresay the old Grand Duke knew who would make a good ruler and who would not," he said. "Your foreign uncle sounds a muddler to me."

He always called them "your foreign uncle" and

"your foreign cousins" and this annoyed Catherine, who felt more at home with them than with her English relations.

She did not know Giles well because it was not till her great-aunt had died, last spring, that she had gone to live with the Hawthornes in their big London house. Aunt Eleanor was her father's sister. Giles was at Eton and often went away in the holidays to stay with friends. He had two grown-up married sisters, but he was the only son. Although he was a month or two younger than Catherine, he was taller than she was, a self-confident, active, intelligent boy, brown-haired and grey-eyed, and, it seemed to Catherine, determined to know better than herself about everything.

Catherine was shy, rather thin, with straight brown hair and ordinary brown eyes; her eyebrows lifted at the ends: it was her only noticeable feature. But under her quietness were strong feelings, which she had first become aware of that time in Letzenstein in January 1848. In April that year she had expected to go back for her uncle Constant's wedding, but her great-aunt's death had prevented it. Afterwards there were so many revolutions in Europe that Sir Walter Hawthorne would not allow her to go abroad.

This year there were revolutions in Italy but northern Europe appeared to have settled down and so the Hawthornes decided that it would be the proper thing to take Catherine to visit her uncle. But they travelled without hurry. Constant Waldemar might be a Grand Duke, but it was of a very small country.

"I don't believe it's as big as an English county,"

Giles had said, when he saw it on a map. He had decided Letzenstein was a joke before he had ever been there.

"Well, even in a county a lot can go on," Catherine had said then. "And Letzenstein is truly a country, with its own people and traditions."

Now, when Giles teased her about the foreign uncle he knew she was fond of, Catherine refused to be drawn into argument. She drank her lemonade in silence, gazing out at the river.

Seeing that she would not rise to his teasing Giles dropped it and looked about him. Presently he said, "What funny people one sees in foreign places. Look at that artist over there—he looks like a tramp, a regular scarecrow. Drawing people for the price of a drink, I suppose, as he's just sent his little boy over to another table with a sketch and they're giving him some money."

Catherine looked round and saw, some distance off, the back of the artist, who sat at a table by himself with a drawing block under his hand. Something about that thin back and big black hat looked very familiar.

"Can it be?" said Catherine, jumping up. "I believe it is!"

She went quickly across, threading her way through the tables so as to come out in front of him. And there was that unmistakable long narrow face with the close-set startlingly blue eyes.

"Rafael!" Catherine cried joyfully, running up to him.

"What? Is it Catherine? Here in Trier? What a nice surprise!" He spoke in English, but with an accent. He flung out his arm and pulled her close with an affectionate hug. "But Catherine, how tall! Like a young lady, almost. What a long time, *chérie,* since I saw you."

Catherine was smiling; at the same time she felt she was nearly crying. "Oh, Raf, it is *so* long!" she said. "But why are you in Trier, not in Letzenstein?"

"I'm on my way home from Venice," he said. "And if you wonder why it is I come through the German states, it is because a kind German going to Cologne brought us from Switzerland for nothing, in his own carriage."

It was such a typical way for Rafael to travel that Catherine began to laugh. Then she became aware that Giles had come up and was staring at Rafael with suspicion, not to say hostility.

"Who is this, may I ask?" he said in his clear English voice.

"It's Rafael le Marre," Catherine said. "One of the cousins, the one who is an artist; he found me when I was lost in the riot, in the snow. Raf, this is my English cousin Giles Hawthorne."

"And he is English!" said Rafael, smiling at Giles. "How very English!"

Catherine had forgotten about the little boy Giles had seen, but now he came up, glancing at them from a pair of lively hazel eyes, and held out a grubby hand to Rafael, with a silver and a copper coin in the palm.

"The penny is for me, the lady gave it to me for myself." It was another English voice.

"Keep it then, Toby," said Rafael. He hailed a waiter by name and called out an order in German. "Dinner for Toby!" he said in English. "Now we have money to pay for it." He spun the silver coin and then gave it to the waiter as he came up with a plate of meat for the child.

The little boy climbed on to a chair and set to. Then he looked up. "*Ma, Raffaelle, niente per te?*" he said.

"I am not yet too hungry," said Rafael. "And first I must draw someone else to earn the money. Eat, Toby, eat all there."

"Why did he speak in Italian?" Catherine asked. "He sounded English."

"He is English," said Rafael. "That's why I brought him along. I found him running wild in Venice. His papa went away in a ship and came not back, he says. He was left with a grandmother, but she too is gone."

"*La nonna* went to the hospital and never came out," said the child, glancing at Catherine from under his thatch of fair hair. "Anthony Reynolds is my name but I'm called Toby. I'm six."

Giles said, "How could you be in Venice recently? It's been held by Italian revolutionaries all the summer against the Austrians."

"Not revolutionaries—republicans," said Rafael. "Yes, you have it right, Giles. We have been besieged and that was no joke, I can tell you. We have held out longer than the Roman Republic. But now the end is coming for the Republic of San Marco, I fear."

"*Evviva Venezia!*" piped up Toby.

"Toby is a patriotic Venetian," said Rafael, smiling. "And I too. They are a brave people."

Suddenly, at a table a little way off, two men began

shouting at each other. Everyone turned round to look. A man and his wife, sitting at a table, were being abused by a youth who was standing up, leaning over it towards them. The attacked man jumped angrily to his feet, knocking over his chair. He shouted in German; the young man was shouting in Italian.

"*Peste!* It's Gaetano!" said Rafael. He put his hand on the table and got up. He walked through between the tables, moving awkwardly, but quite fast.

"No stick!" Catherine cried, in surprise, for when she had known him before Rafael was recovering from an accident in which he had injured his back and nearly always used a stick to help himself balance.

He heard her cry and glanced back at her with a smile. "I'm better, you see!" he said.

Toby seized the bone from his dish and ran after him. Catherine followed, not heeding Giles's protest.

The young Italian was beside himself with rage. Catherine had always thought of Italians as dark, but Gaetano had a mop of curly tawny hair and grey eyes; she thought he looked as beautiful and as arrogant as a renaissance prince.

"*Basta*, Gaetano! *Basta!*" cried Rafael, as he approached. "Enough! Stop now." He laid his hand on the young man's shoulder. Gaetano shook it off.

The shouting match now became three-sided, almost four-sided, since Rafael joined in with Italian to Gaetano and German to the man he was abusing. If Catherine had not known he was trying to stop the quarrel she would have thought Rafael was taking the most active part in it. This was just what Sir Walter Hawthorne thought as he came to pick up the children and saw his niece apparently involved in an international incident.

"Catherine!" he said in shocked tones, coming up behind her. "Come with me at once."

And he took her arm and hurried her away, Giles falling in beside him. Catherine twisted half round but Rafael had not noticed. Toby had, though, and she called out to him, "Toby! We are staying at the Hotel Imperial."

She saw Toby nod before she was scolded anew by her uncle.

"What do you mean by telling that little beggar where we are staying?" he demanded. "Have you taken leave of your senses?"

"But that's my cousin Rafael le Marre—not the boy, the man with dark hair," Catherine said, for Raf's broad-brimmed hat had fallen off and was hanging by its strings at his back. His dark thick hair stood up in a crest on his head.

Sir Walter swung round. "What! That fellow with a week's beard?" he said. "He doesn't look the sort of person I should wish you to associate with. Come along."

And he firmly hurried Catherine away from the scene.

Giles told his father of the meeting. "And he's been with the Italian revolutionaries all the summer, in Venice. That young man is probably one of them. But the little boy is English."

"We don't want to get mixed up in a public quarrel," said Sir Walter. "That would not do at all."

Lady Hawthorne, when she heard of the incident,

was surprised at her shy niece's involving herself. But it confirmed views she had already formed of this foreign cousin of Catherine's.

"Altogether an undesirable character," she said, as they sat at dinner later that evening. "It is true he is the Grand Duke's cousin, since their fathers were half-brothers. But his mother was a nobody; it was a morganatic marriage and she was never recognized at the Letzenstein court after the restoration in 1815. Although his father was Grand Duke, the son inherited nothing. His uncle, Grand Duke Edmond, took him into his household but he turned out badly, ran away and lived in Italy, threw in his lot with the revolutionaries long ago."

Aunt Eleanor always knew everything about people; everything, thought Catherine, but what they were really like. "Raf's not a revolutionary," she said.

"Raf?" said her uncle, with a chuckle. "Good name for him! Never seen such a raffish fellow in my life!"

As they left the dining room one of the waiters attracted Catherine's attention. She thought he was retrieving something she had dropped and turned back. But he handed her a crumpled note with a glance that counselled secrecy.

Catherine immediately recognized Rafael's pointed foreign writing and held the note inside her hand.

Lady Hawthorne, who had rested in the afternoon, now wished to take a stroll outside in the warm summer evening and was waiting for Adèle, her French maid, to bring her wrap. But when Catherine said she was tired her aunt told her she might go upstairs at once. "But do not retire for half an hour after eating," she admonished her. Aunt Eleanor had decided opinions on health, digestion and behaviour.

Catherine meekly climbed the stairs, passing Adèle on the way. To her the Parisienne was a formidable person who, she felt, disapproved of her as the worst kind of English miss, shy, thin and unfashionable—so unlike her aunt, a stately figure, always dressed well and never at a loss. Eleanor Ayre had been older than her brother Robert, Catherine's father. She and Sir Walter were both middle-aged, imposing, distinguished people.

Catherine went into her bedroom, turned up the lamp and opened Rafael's note. Since he spoke English mostly by ear, his command of the written language was eccentric. He had written this note with a black crayon.

Catherine my dier, can I see you one moment? I wait you in the glass house of plants.

Raf

Catherine sighed with relief to think her uncle and aunt had gone out; she could go to the conservatory without exciting any notice. But she waited till she heard Adèle pass her door on her way back to Lady Hawthorne's room before she went downstairs again.

A few of the guests, none English, were in the conservatory. Rafael was sitting on a seat there. A long thin person, he looked even longer and thinner with his legs stretched out, leaning back with his eyes shut; evidently, waiting for Catherine, he had fallen asleep. She thought he looked very tired. She went and sat down beside him and he woke up at once.

"Catherine, you come! Excellent!" he said, sitting up straight.

"I didn't like to go away and leave you in that quarrel," Catherine said. "But Uncle Walter made me. What happened?"

"Oh, I made Gaetano apologize in the end," said Rafael. "Silly boy! Quite harmless Austrians they were and he must attack them as if they were responsible for the siege of Venice. What a problem are these national feelings! At home Austrians are nice people, but in Italy they are not wanted."

"Who is Gaetano?" Catherine asked.

"Gaetano? He is the younger brother of Silvia— Gaetano Frasca," said Raf. "Silvia is the wife of my friend Luca Caravelli, who has been a patriotic writer in Venice. He uses the name '*Bucintoro*' for his political writings. You know what is *Bucintoro*, Catherine? It was the great ship of Venice, which Napoleon burned when he took the city. Luca, he sends off paper fleets to attack the Austrian imperialists!" He smiled. "And they don't like it! They pay Luca the compliment of wishing to arrest him. He has been long in exile, in London. But when in Venice they declared a new Republic of San Marco, he went back and took an honoured place under Daniele Manin. But alas Venice cannot hold out much longer and that is why it was necessary to get Luca away before it fell."

"Is that what you've been doing, Raf? Escaping again?" said Catherine.

He laughed. "Yes! Again!" he said. "Silvia brought their little girl all the way to Letzenstein to ask my help, because she could not persuade Luca to leave. That was before the siege. Last May, I got there, and at once it began. Then poor Luca, he got the cholera. There was much cholera, and famine. And not till nearly the end would he try to escape. Well! Nor should I, in his place. But at last we got away, thanks be to God. This morning we arrive here in Trier. But now we have no money to go on. It came to me that perhaps your Uncle would take us into Letzenstein."

Catherine felt very doubtful of this. "He's a diplomat," she said, "And he's always afraid of getting implicated in incidents. Besides, he didn't approve of you, Raf."

"Why didn't he approve of me?" said Rafael. "Did he think perhaps I was making that quarrel at the café?"

Catherine did not like to repeat what her relations had said about him. Instead she said, "But you can have my money, Raf. I haven't much, but Aunt Eleanor told me to carry it with me always, so here it is."

She got out her little purse, shook all the coins into her hand and held them out to him.

Rafael hesitated. "I don't like to take your money, Catherine," he said. "But there's Toby—he must eat."

"Toby seemed to be doing all right," said Catherine. "What about you? Did you have any dinner?"

"Well, no . . . After Gaetano's nonsense there was no chance to earn any more by drawing people," said Rafael. "To-morrow I can."

"Take it—you must take it, please," Catherine said earnestly and put the money into his hand.

Rafael did take it. As he put the coins in his pocket he said, "Ah! There is my friend Luca. I was hoping to introduce him to your uncle. The English are sympathetic to the Italians wishing for independence."

Catherine saw a man standing on the threshold, hesitantly gazing about him. He had a striking head, with thick dark hair beginning to go grey, a pale face with a heavy fold each side of his mouth and large brown eyes.

As she caught sight of him, Catherine had a fleeting impression of someone going quickly out of the door; she almost thought it was Giles. But surely Giles had gone out with his parents?

Then Luca Caravelli saw Rafael's waving hand and came towards them. When Catherine was introduced, he kissed her hand.

"Sit down, Luca," said Rafael. "Sir Walter Hawthorne is out, so we wait." He pronounced the name as "Autorne."

Luca smiled. "You don't pronounce correctly the English aspirates, Rafael," he said. "It is *Hawth*orne."

Catherine was surprised at his good pronunciation and said so.

"The fruit of exile!" he said. "I have lived in London. I have worked in the British Museum. But still, I am not perfect in English. I have a writer's ear, so I can tell I do not altogether catch the phrasing, the lilt. But the aspirates, I have learned!"

"*H*aut-*h*one," said Rafael, making another shot and when they laughed he complained, "What is the matter with Englishmen these days? Why are they not all called Pitt and Fox as they used to be?"

Catherine, laughing, said, "Your names are just as hard to us."

"What is hard about le Marre?" he retorted. "Except that you are faint-hearted about that double R!"

They went on to talk of the escape from Venice. Luca Caravelli told more than Rafael, perhaps because he felt they owed their escape to him. "With him, we passed as Frenchmen," he said. "His artist's things assisted too. Everyone expects artists to be mad, to get caught in sieges and yet not be belligerent. Gaetano and I, we had to keep our mouths shut, but that is no difficulty with Raf, for he is happy to talk for all, in almost any language!"

"No difficulty! It's the devil's own job to make Gaetano keep his mouth shut," said Rafael. "He has only to hear one word of German to go off like a bottle of champagne. You should have heard him this afternoon! And I don't think he forgives me for talking German myself, but this after all is one of my mother tongues—my father-tongue, perhaps I should say. French is my mother!"

They were laughing again when Sir Walter and Lady Hawthorne walked into the conservatory, piloted by Giles. So it must have been Giles she had seen, Catherine thought.

Sir Walter was annoyed. Although Luca Caravelli rose at once and Rafael as soon as he could, he ignored them and addressed his niece. "Catherine, I told you I did not wish you to associate with this person. Why have you disobeyed me?"

"I didn't know you wanted me to refuse to see Rafael," Catherine faltered. "And anyway, Uncle Walter, I shall see him in Letzenstein."

"I sincerely hope not!" said Sir Walter, irritably.

"I do not understand this," said Rafael. "Why, please, am I not to see Catherine? I too am almost an uncle, a cousin of her uncle Constant Waldemar."

"I don't wish to have a scene," said Sir Walter. "Whether you are related or not, I cannot allow my niece to associate with someone who looks like a tramp, talks like a revolutionary, and behaves like a cad."

"Cat?" said Rafael, puzzled.

Even in the stress of the moment, Catherine had to giggle.

"Cad," said Luca. "This is an English term of abuse for someone whose conduct is dishonourable."

Sir Walter looked at the Italian in some surprise. Luca's English and the fact that, unlike Rafael, he looked shaved and clean, did not fit into the picture he had formed of a disreputable artist and his friends.

"What have I done dishonourable?" demanded Rafael, with a blue flash in his eye, and suddenly he looked much more like the last of the le Marres, the old Grand Ducal family of Letzenstein, than a wandering artist.

"If you don't consider it dishonourable to take money from a child, you have curious standards of honour," said Sir Walter colder.

"I gave it to him! He didn't ask for it," Catherine said earnestly. "Oh, please, Uncle Walter—he hasn't had any dinner today. They've used up all their money escaping from Venice." She turned to Rafael, who had thrust his hand into his pocket. "If you don't keep it I shall cry—I shall cry all night." She was nearly crying now.

Rafael, who had been looking angry, smiled and

bent to give her a kiss. "Cry not, *chérie*," he said. "I will feast on your present and we shall meet over the river soon. I see it will not do to ask a favour from your English uncle. *Tant pis!* We will walk to Felsenbourg, will we not, Luca? So! Goodnight, goodnight to you all." He bowed to Lady Hawthorne, took his friend's arm and walked away.

Catherine turned on Giles. "Was it you? Giles! You spied on us."

"I did not!" he retorted. "I came in here and saw him taking your pocket money. Whether you offered it or not, he should not have taken it, should he, Papa?"

"Of course not," said Sir Walter. "Shocking behaviour."

"Oh, why can't you understand?" Catherine said, tears pricking in her eyes. "They had to get out of Venice or Signor Caravelli would have been arrested by the Austrians. Raf spent the only shilling he had on dinner for Toby. Giles, you saw that yourself."

"Catherine, you are overwrought," said Aunt Eleanor. "Now, go quietly up to bed, there's a good child."

It was no use arguing. Catherine said a choked goodnight and ran up the stairs. She was crying by the time she reached her room. But once alone, she soon calmed down. After all, Rafael had kept her money, so he would not starve. In Letzenstein it would be different. There, he was not only the cousin of the Grand Duke but his friend, almost like a brother to him. Her aunt and uncle would have to accept him then. Thinking how surprised they would be to discover his real position, she began to smile, and so went to bed cheerful.

2

Some Kind of Incident

NEXT DAY THE Hawthornes started for Letzenstein. Catherine wondered if her uncle had speeded his departure to avoid that undesirable acquaintance, Rafael le Marre. He had not seemed in a hurry to leave historic Trier before. Anyway, off they went, the family travelling in a big closed carriage hired in Brussels and Adèle, the French maid, with the English manservant Wilcox, and the luggage, in another vehicle of less consequence. There would hardly have been room, Catherine thought, for Rafael, with his Italian friends and Toby.

For a little way the Moselle, tributary of the Rhine, was the frontier between Letzenstein and the Germanies, so that they only had to cross it to reach the country, but then they had a further drive to the capital, Felsenbourg, which was situated to the southwest, in the arm of another curling river which ran into the Moselle and so into the great Rhine.

They passed through the uplands of Letzenstein, through fertile valleys where vines and orchards grew up the hillsides. Castles perched in commanding positions, villages nestled in sheltered corners. Harvesting was going on; carts piled high with yellow sheaves of corn trundled along the dusty roads, impeding their progress. Everyone was busy but nobody seemed in a hurry.

"Pretty country," pronounced Lady Hawthorne. Catherine was glad that Letzenstein at least had her aunt's approval.

Travelling in leisurely style they had luncheon at an inn and arrived in Felsenbourg early in the afternoon. No exact date had been named for their visit to begin and it seemed more convenient to arrive after, rather than just before, a meal.

Felsenbourg was built on a rocky promontory looped by a river, its tall gabled houses crowded together, and the road was steep, in spite of its zig-zag bends. But at last they reached the wide square in front of the Grand Ducal palace, which Catherine remembered so well from her earlier visit. And now, to her surprise, it was once more full of people, though not a howling mob but a crowd in holiday mood. They were watching a parade of soldiers. The carriage came to a stop, unable to proceed further.

"Oh, there's Con!" said Catherine. "Taking the salute."

Her uncle was in his dark green Chasseurs uniform, with a peaked gold-braided cap, and he was on a big black horse in front of the tall iron railings which screened the palace.

"Well, we have a good view from here," said Lady Hawthorne. "We had better wait till it is over."

Giles watched with interest; he was thinking of going into the British army, if he did not decide on a diplomatic career like his father. "They're not bad," he announced. "Smartly turned out."

Catherine presently noticed a disturbance in the corner of the square near them; a procession of working men was trying to battle its way through, carrying banners, though Catherine could not read what was written on them. Civil Guards were trying to keep them back. The Grand Duke had not seen them; they were to one side of him.

Catherine said nothing but presently Sir Walter's attention was caught. "What's going on over there?" he said. "Looks like a demonstration. I hope there won't be an incident."

Sir Walter Hawthorne spent his life avoiding incidents. Alas for his peace of mind! He had scarcely spoken when there was a loud report.

The Grand Duke's horse reared up; he lost his seat and fell off.

Catherine shrieked. Before she knew what she was doing she had opened the carriage door and jumped out. Someone had shot Con! She pushed between the people ahead and came out into the open space left for the parade.

Then she saw Con scrambling to his feet. Other horses were plunging about; two grooms had run to control his. Con at once went over, spoke to them and to the horse, which was quieting down.

At the sound of the shot the crowd had given a collective groan, like a football crowd, and a shout when Con got up again.

Then a man picked up something from the ground and held it up. He shouted something and Catherine saw Con laughing. Then everybody began to laugh. "*C'est un feu d'artifice!*" said someone near her.

A firework! It was not a shot at all. In her relief, Catherine began to laugh too. Everybody was cheering now, and clapping.

Now that he was standing, hatless, on the ground, Constant suddenly caught sight of the men with banners, still pushing on against the Civil Guards. He immediately walked over towards them, pursued by anxious officers and secretaries. A tall man, with a rugged face, Con walked with a long stride, easily outdistancing them.

Directly commanded by their Grand Duke to fall back, the Civil Guards had to obey. The leaders of the procession formed up anew and one made a short speech and handed to Con a scroll of paper. He took it and replied; they all spoke in the Letzensteiner German which Catherine did not know.

As he turned away from the demonstrators Constant saw Catherine standing by herself in front of the spectators.

"Catherine!" he said in surprise, coming over to her. "Alone? What has happened?"

"Oh, Con, I thought you were shot!" she cried, running to him.

Con caught her up so that her feet left the ground and kissed her on both cheeks.

"Bless you, my niece! It was nothing but a firecracker!" he said, and he spoke English well, better than Rafael, for when he had been exiled by his father he had spent some years in Canada and long before that he had studied at Oxford.

"My uncle's carriage is just here," she said. "We couldn't get through the crowd."

Sir Walter Hawthorne had opened the door of his carriage and was standing on the step, looking over the heads of the intervening people. Giles was already pushing his way through them.

But before he arrived a woman and a boy came hurrying towards Con. The boy was running and waving a letter. He could not say a word, he was so out of breath. He was a slim boy, a little taller than Catherine, with a mop of long straight light brown hair and eyes of a much darker brown, set in black lashes.

Now the woman came up. She was tall and strong, with a face that reminded Catherine of an antique statue, carved on straight and simple lines. She looked about thirty and wore a plain brown dress; she had no hat on her thick dark red hair, coiled up in a net on her neck. She curtsied to the Grand Duke.

"Jeanne! What can I do for you?" Con said, speaking in French.

"It's in the letter Paul gave you, sir," she answered, in the same language. Catherine understood it better than she had at the time of her first visit; affection for her mother's country had given her an incentive to learn it. "It's about a child who needs an eye-operation," this woman said. "We would be grateful for help with the expenses. I wrote by post but perhaps you did not get it."

"My secretaries always weed out the wrong things," Con said. "Certainly I will help, Jeanne. Have you any news of Rafael?"

She shook her head and Catherine suddenly realized

who she was: Jeanne d'Estel, the dancer, who had married Rafael le Marre last summer.

"It looks as if that republic in Venice can't last much longer," said Con. "I hope Raf will get out all right."

"*Mais oui*," Catherine joined in eagerly, in her best French. "I've just seen him in Trier."

"Trier?" cried Con and Jeanne, in surprise, both together.

Catherine began to explain but at that moment Sir Walter Hawthorne advanced upon them. "We seem to have arrived at an inopportune moment, sir," he said. "Some kind of incident, I'm afraid."

Con smiled. "Some joker threw a firecracker!" he said. "My thoughts were elsewhere. My wife is having a baby, her first child." He looked back towards the palace. "I wonder how she is?"

"A *very* inopportune moment," Sir Walter said, looking surprised and embarrassed.

"And there was some muddle over two rival events," Con went on. "There was the review of the bodyguard and then there was this petition about the municipal elections. I'd forgotten—or had never been told—they were on the same day. However, I've now got the petition firsthand, instead of via every conceivable office and official, so perhaps I can do something about it, for once. You know, sir, the smaller the country, the more complicated the process of ruling it!"

Officers and secretaries now interrupted them and Con told them he would have to leave them. "Get them to take you inside and I'll hope to see you soon."

He waved to Catherine, smiling, and walked off,

still hatless, his rough dark hair on end and dust from the ground marking his green uniform.

"What a funny sort of Grand Duke!" observed Giles and Catherine knew from his scornful tone that he did not think much of her uncle.

"He's a very good Grand Duke for us," said the boy with dark eyes, in good English. "We don't need a pompous dignified person."

Catherine had not noticed they were still there, standing back from the group but able to hear what passed. Now Jeanne said to her, in hesitant English, "Please! Tell me, you see Rafael in Trier?"

Catherine began to tell of their meeting but Jeanne soon turned helplessly to the boy. "*Paul, tu dois traduire pour moi.*"

"She wants me to translate," Paul explained. "Tell me, and I'll tell her."

But Sir Walter Hawthorne very quickly put a stop to this conversation, firmly taking his niece's arm. "Catherine, come along. You cannot talk to all these people."

"But she's Rafael's wife," said Catherine. "She wants to know if he's all right."

Sir Walter, however, hurried her all the more. "We don't want to get mixed up with them," he said.

"Is that their son?" Giles asked.

Catherine laughed. "No! They only got married last summer. I don't know who he is . . . or, wait! He must be the boy Rafael fetched from Paris during the February Revolution there last year. Raf is his guardian. That's when he found Jeanne again, climbing over a barricade, he told me in a letter. He had lost her, you see, when she thought he was dead and gave up dancing to be a nurse to the poor people in Paris."

Aunt Eleanor heard the end of this history, as they reached the carriage. She looked shocked but peered out and saw Jeanne le Marre still gazing after Catherine. "A dancer!" she said, in disapproving tones. "And she's not wearing a bonnet!" This, it seemed, was almost as great a solecism to Lady Hawthorne's sense of propriety as being a theatrical performer.

"Don't you think she is beautiful, in a special sort of way?" Catherine said. "I once saw a watercolour sketch of her that Raf had done. She looks older now, of course."

"I don't think she is a suitable person for you to know, Catherine," said Aunt Eleanor, folding her lips primly.

Catherine sighed. All her favourite people seemed to be unsuitable.

At least no one could say the Grand Duke was unsuitable, though the Hawthornes could, and did, say that he did not have the correct manner for his position. Although they considered Letzenstein unimportant, they still expected its ruler to behave according to the acceptable pattern for royalty. As Giles put it, "Grand Dukes ought to be grand." Giles thought Constant Waldemar had looked a fool in the firecracker incident.

The first person Catherine met in the palace was her governess Miss Lacey. It had been a disappointment to Miss Lacey to miss the tour through the German cities but she had been detained in England by a sister's illness. She had come by train from Ostend repeating the journey she had made with Catherine on the first visit to Letzenstein, and had arrived late the day before. She and Catherine were in the same rooms on the second floor, with Giles near them, but Sir Walter and Lady Hawthorne were on the first, best, floor.

Catherine looked out of the window and saw flowers in formal beds beyond the terrace and she remembered that snow had covered everything last time. "It seems almost a different place in summer," she said.

Boom!

"That's a gun," said Giles.

Boom!

"What can it be?" Catherine was fearful; revolutions were associated with this palace, in her mind.

Boom!

They went out into the passage and along to the grand staircase, looking down into the gallery that ran across the front of the building, with tall casement windows opening on to a balcony.

"There's Con," Catherine said, seeing her uncle come out of a room on the floor below. She ran down the stairs as another boom sounded outside. "Con! What's that? That noise like a gun?"

"They're firing a salute," he said, smiling. "For the birth of my son."

"Oh! The baby is born!" she cried, delighted. "Is Yolande all right?"

"Yes, but she is tired," said Con. "They say he is a big baby, though he looks pretty small to me! I expect you can see then both tomorrow." He looked at his watch. "I must go. You can amuse yourself here, can't you, Catherine? Take your cousin to see the town. Miss Lacey, perhaps, will go with you."

Miss Lacey was just behind and she said, "Certainly, sir," quite eagerly. But she insisted that they should first put on walking shoes and hats and that Catherine should take a light coat because, she said, "It is not so hot once evening draws in."

Evening had not drawn very near when they started; it was still warm and the sun shone in a clear sky. When they began to walk about Felsenbourg Catherine realized how little she knew of it.

"I wasn't allowed out much, you see," she explained to Giles. "Because of the danger of revolution."

Giles found it hard to believe in a revolution in Letzenstein. Its capital city was no bigger than the German provincial towns they had seen and much smaller than Brussels. In the August evening there was an air of relaxation; people were sitting at little tables outside the café in the square. Nobody was in a hurry. The Felsenburgers were homely people, Giles thought, and did not look as if they could get excited about anything.

Miss Lacey had a guide book in her hand and pointed out buildings of interest. From the Square outside the palace where the government ministries were, they went into Old Schools Square, where the university and the opera house faced each other across the cobbles and then they walked round the old walls, looking down on a wide boulevarde below and further down over higgledy piggledy roofs to the wharves and the river.

"And that's where I was lost in the riot, and Rafael found me," Catherine thought, staring down. Brass on the boats passing twinkled, the waves sparkled in the golden light. The past seemed almost like a dream, the past of snow and darkness and revolution.

They came down from the wall into St. Michael's Square, where the old north gate of the city stood. Near it was the church and house of the order of the Star of St. Michael, Letzenstein's order of honour, founded in the crusades. On the front of the Knights' House was a medieval wooden carving of the Archangel, in knight's armour, in the act of slaying a small but vicious dragon. Miss Lacey and Catherine knew all about this; Giles, rather tired of being informed by them, stopped to look at a tall old inn by the gateway. Its sign, painted on a board hung on an iron spear above the door, showed another angel in a swirling white robe, standing on clouds in the sky, blowing on a long, thin medieval trumpet, gilded like his hair and golden breastplate.

"That's not St. Michael, is it?" he said.

"Could it be the Angel Gabriel, blowing the trumpet for the Last Judgement?" Catherine wondered. "You know, the Handel anthem 'The trumpet shall sound—and the dead shall be raised'?" The tremendous music sounded in her head. Miss Lacey observed, "That would suit St. Michael quite well, as in medieval paintings he's often represented weighing the souls of the dead."

"*After* finally killing the Dragon, I suppose," said Giles, with one of his supercilious smiles.

Suddenly Catherine caught sight of a familiar gnome-like figure in the doorway. "Agnes! she cried. "Miss Lacey, I'm sure it's Agnes!"

Agnes was the English cockney maid, married to

Alphonse Bertholet, who had looked after them in the palace.

Agnes heard her and came hurrying towards them. "Well, I never!" she said. "My, haven't you growed tall, miss? I heard you was coming but I didn't reckon to see you so soon. Did you wonder why I wasn't in the palace to greet you? Well, Alphonse and me has gone into business again. It was the Prince's doing—Grand Duke, I mean—I never can get used to that. He was so grateful to Alphonse for helping to rescue Monsieur Rafael from the cellars that he would get us this place, for reward."

"So you're living here? Running it?" Catherine said. "Do you like it?"

"Oh, there's nothing to beat inn life, if you're used to it," said Agnes. "Always something on! But it's a bit of a headache being the Madame, I can tell you. Chivvying the chambermaids and all that. I said to Alphonse, when we was deciding, 'I haven't the style for managing an hotel,' I said, but an honest to goodness inn, well, I'd have a shot at that. I reckon he was a bit disappointed, because Alphonse has style, you know, having been a waiter in big places. Still, he likes the Angel because lots of old friends come along here. It's a friendly place."

Giles was gazing at Agnes in astonishment. He had never met anyone like her in his life. His parents' servants would never have talked to them like this. Miss Lacey had never considered Agnes's style quite the thing but she was grateful for past cups of tea in a foreign land.

"I'm so glad to hear you are comfortably settled,

Agnes," she said. "Now, we are just going to look at the church."

"Oh, it's shut for repairs," said Agnes. "They've got a new Archbishop here and he's busy tidying everything up, churches and people too. Everyone used to grumble at the old man but now he's died they say he was a saint in comparison with this one."

Catherine laughed. She remembered the old Archbishop, a courtly relic of an age gone by, but more worldly than saintly. Then just as she was laughing she caught sight of Rafael and his friends coming through the gate. Gaetano was carrying Toby on his back.

"Oh! They've got here!" she cried and ran over to them. "Raf! Hullo!"

"So! Almost we caught you up, Catherine," Rafael said cheerfully. He was covered in dust; they all were.

"But you can't have walked all the way from Trier," said Catherine.

"No, we got many rides, mostly in farm carts," Raf said. "No one was going to Xandeln, so we had to come to Felsenbourg. I thought we could stay with Alphonse all right." He waved to Agnes, who waved back and ran indoors.

Gaetano put Toby down and they all walked across to the Angel Inn. Rafael had his stick, Catherine noticed, and he sat down on one of the benches outside the inn as if he felt too tired to stand any longer.

"The last bit is always the worst, isn't it?" he said. "We started last night, as we had nowhere to sleep in Trier."

"I hope you had something to eat," said Catherine anxiously.

"We bought much bread with your money, *chèrie,* and some cheese and a bottle of good old *vin ordinaire,*" said Rafael. "So! We live, thanks to you!"

Giles was standing looking at him, with his hands in his pockets.

"Giles is hanging on to his pocket money," said Rafael, with a smile. "He thinks it's not safe when I turn up!"

Just then Jeanne came out of the inn, with Agnes behind her.

"Jeanne?" cried Rafael, so surprised to see her there that he jumped to his feet and nearly lost his balance.

Jeanne caught his arms and steadied him, and then kissed him. "Oh, Raf, *mon cher!*" was all she could say at first.

They sat down on the bench together and he introduced Luca Caravelli and Gaetano Frasca. Jeanne talked in French but Catherine could follow quite well now. She told Luca that his wife Silvia was with her in Felsenbourg.

"Indeed, it is for her sake I am here and not in Xandeln, as Raf expected," she said. "For we came to consult a specialist about your little girl's eye, and it seems they can now do an operation which may save the sight of it."

"But that is wonderful," Luca said, his tired face lighting up. "And Silvia? She is here?"

"Here she comes," said Jeanne.

Silvia Caravelli came running out of the inn. She was younger than Jeanne, a small neat person with a golden skin and smooth hair the colour of dark honey. Reunited with her husband and brother after so many anxious months, she began to weep, silent tears running down her cheeks.

Then Alphonse Bertholet, a stout little man with big moustaches, came out carrying a tray of glasses. He was bursting with welcoming phrases in several languages as he filled them with wine and handed them round.

Toby seized a glass off the tray, drank a mouthful and then coughed.

"Serves you right!" Raf said. He leaned over, picked up the water carafe and poured a dollop into Toby's glass.

A very small girl in a long white nightgown appeared on the doorstep, calling out, "Mámma! Mámma!" There was a white film across one dark eye.

"Cataract," murmured Miss Lacey. "Unusual in a child."

"Oh, Chiara!" cried her mother Silvia. But it was Luca who ran and picked her up, kissing her many times. "*Carina, carina!*" he said, hugging his little girl and putting her on his knee when he sat down.

"Ha! A wife for me!" cried Toby, excitedly.

They all began to laugh.

"Toby won't be left out," said Rafael. He started to tell Jeanne about Toby, in French.

Miss Lacey cleared her throat. "Catherine, we must go home," she said.

"Miss Lacey! How are you?" Rafael said, rising to shake her hand. "So many people here, I had not recognized you. Well, you must come back tomorrow with Catherine. Giles too, if he wish."

So they had to go, Catherine unwillingly. She looked

back as they left the square and saw them all sitting outside the inn talking, and Alphonse and Agnes standing and talking too. Toby was kneeling on the bench beside Raf, eating cheese biscuits; Rafael had his arm round Jeanne; and Silvia, her tears dried, was asking Luca a hundred questions in rapid Italian while Chiara, excited, jumped up and down on his knee. Gaetano did more answering than Luca.

"Monsieur le Marre does seem to get mixed up in revolutions, doesn't he?" said Miss Lacey, who had never felt Rafael was quite a respectable character. "Even marriage hasn't settled him down. But then I understand his wife was an actress."

Catherine feared that Miss Lacey, like Aunt Eleanor, thought that Jeanne was, if possible, even more unsuitable than Rafael.

Giles said, "I suppose you didn't know, Miss Lacey, but my parents don't want Catherine to know those people."

"Dear me," said Miss Lacey. "But as Monsieur le Marre is the Grand Duke's cousin and friend, I am afraid the acquaintance can hardly be avoided."

Catherine smiled. She could not help being pleased at Giles's evident annoyance with Miss Lacey's mildly corrective tone. Giles saw her smile and he scowled and remained sulkily silent for the rest of their walk home. It was plain that he was determined to maintain his critical attitude to Catherine's foreign cousins.

∽ 3 ∽

Princes and Peasants

NEXT MORNING Con took Catherine to visit his wife Yolande and the new baby. Yolande was lying in bed with her shining red-gold hair in two thick long plaits. The baby was beside her in a cradle on a stand. Catherine peeped at him; his eyes were tight shut and a crest of dark hair with a reddish glint stood up along the middle of his head. Catherine thought his skin looked loose, as if he hadn't quite settled into it yet.

"I've never seen such a new baby before," she said.

"Only to think this is his first sunrise," said Yolande.

Catherine asked what his name would be.

"Well, we think Christian Louis," said Con. "Yolande's father was Louis, and Christian was the name of several earlier Grand Dukes—le Marres, of course. I would like to call him Rafael as well and ask Raf to be his godfather. But I'm not sure Yolande doesn't think having Raf for a godfather would not make a changeling out of him!"

Yolande laughed. "What nonsense!" she said. "Just because I said Rafael was more of an anxiety to Con than an aid—going off to every revolution that blows up!"

"Well, these Italians have good cause to be glad he went to Venice," said Con. He told Catherine that he had visited the inn late last night; he had seen Rafael and Jeanne, though not their Italian friends. "And Raf has picked up another orphan child," he said to Yolande.

"Hasn't he got enough of them at Xandeln already?" Yolande said, amused. "Well, we shall see them all soon, when we go down for our long-promised holiday."

"Oh! Are we going to Xandeln?" Catherine said, joyfully.

The castle, near the frontier in the north, was the home of Rafael le Marre's ancestors; taken away from him when he was a boy by his uncle, Con's father Grand Duke Edmond, it had been restored by his cousin at his accession. Rafael and Jeanne had made a home there for a fatherless family from the Paris slums and had collected other orphans and some crippled people during the past year. Raf had said he would not live in his castle unless he could fill it with homeless people.

"As soon as I can travel comfortably, we'll go," said Yolande. "I expect your uncle and aunt will be happy to stay there, on the way back to Brussels."

Con had to leave them then but Catherine stayed for a while to talk to Yolande. She heard something of the difficulties Con had had to face since becoming Grand Duke of Letzenstein.

"You see, he never did exile Julius Varenshalt, although

his Altenberg cousins said he should," Yolande explained. "Julius married an Austrian princess—not an imperial princess of course, but of a noble family. He's one of the richest men in Letzenstein because the coal mines in the south are on Varenshalt land. Perhaps that helped the match! Anyway, he has become the leader of those landowners and business men who were frightened by all the revolutions last year, in Paris and Germany and now in Italy."

"But they've all lost," Catherine said. "Even Paris, my uncle Walter says, because President Louis Napoleon is not the sort of republican the revolutionaries wanted."

"Nobody feels sure they've lost for good," said Yolande. "Here, when Con set up a liberal government, all sorts of exiles returned and started a new Republican party. Julius wants it declared illegal but Con says that so long as they keep the law they have a right to organize themselves. I sometimes think Con would like to be a republican himself! He never enjoyed being a prince, poor Con. And now he's caught between Right and Left and nothing he does pleases everybody."

"But people were cheering yesterday when they realized he wasn't shot," said Catherine.

"Thank God I didn't know about that till it was over!" Yolande said. "Yes, indeed, dear Con is popular, of course he is, with the ordinary people. But I hardly know which is more a nuisance to us, Cousin Julius or Jacques Roncard, the Republican leader."

The baby woke up and began to cry. "Oh, listen to him!" said Yolande. "How soon they start and how loud they cry!"

"What shall I do?" asked Catherine nervously.

But just then a nurse came in, picked up the infant in an expert way and gave him to Yolande. He blinked up at her with unfocussed eyes.

"How strange to think he will one day be a great tall man like Con," said Yolande, smoothing the crested hair lovingly.

Catherine presently went back to her rooms. Miss Lacey was not so interested in the new baby as in the expedition they were to make to visit Marienwald, an ancient Abbey which lay south and west of Felsenbourg, towards the border with Valmay, now united to Letzenstein since its Princess's marriage to the Grand Duke. It was in Medlerne, where the Varenshalts were Dukes. The coal mines, Sir Walter said, lay to the southeast.

"Letzenstein would hardly be a visible state without them, in these modern days," he said. "Steel too; that's an old industry here."

It was always interesting travelling with Uncle Walter, Catherine thought, because he knew so much about the history of places. Aunt Eleanor too knew a lot about furniture and paintings; it was she who had planned this visit to the monastery, having heard of their collection of pictures.

It was a very hot day. The closed carriage, smelling of warm leather and bouncing on its springs as they drove along the dusty white road, made Catherine feel a little unwell. She was quite glad when it stopped, even though they had not arrived anywhere.

Sir Walter let down the glass (closed against the

dust) and immediately they became aware of people shouting not far off.

"Dear me! We seem to have run into trouble again," he said. "I can see your monastery, Eleanor, but it's half way up the hill opposite and there's a regular scrum going on by the bridge at the bottom."

Giles looked out of the other window. Then Sir Walter got out; they all got out, Aunt Eleanor putting up her parasol to shield her face from the sun.

The heat was so strong that Catherine felt almost dizzy. From the cloudless blue sky the light blazed on the white road and filled the valley ahead with a slight haze. Catherine blinked. There certainly seemed to be a lot of people and carts at the bottom of the slope, at the top of which the Belgian coachman had halted. The groom held the horses while the coachman descended and came to consult Sir Walter.

"He doesn't know what it's all about but doesn't like the look of it," Uncle Walter told them. "It's a great nuisance to have come so far and then be baulked of our visit."

Aunt Eleanor was very annoyed indeed. "Don't they have any sort of police in this country?" she said. "Is there another route to Marienwald?" It was particularly trying to see the great stone buildings of the monastery across the valley.

This their Belgian driver did not know. Discussion and argument proceeded until Giles said, "Hullo! Here are some gentlemen out shooting."

A small party, with dogs and keepers in attendance, had come out of a lane and were looking down at the scene by the bridge. Then they saw the foreign carriage and two gentlemen, in sporting breeches and jackets, came up to them. Both were young, about thirty, and as they approached Catherine recognized Con's cousin Julius Varenshalt, who had tried so hard, eighteen months ago, to oust him from the succession and himself play the part of Regent for Catherine.

"It's Duke Julius," she whispered to Aunt Eleanor, "the Duke of Medlerne."

Julius was a handsome man, dark, with grey eyes, and his courtly manner appealed to Lady Hawthorne, as Catherine could see. Recognizing Catherine, he had guessed these were her English relations and spoke in English, apologizing for his hesitations. He did not speak it easily, as Con did. He soon discovered where they were bound.

"But you must not go that way now," he said.

"What is happening?" Sir Walter asked, glancing again down the hill.

Duke Julius laughed. "It is nothing! The peasants are angry about this new grain registration scheme. They never like anyone to know what they've got in the barn! I have sympathy with them. Interference by government officials in one's private affairs is a new idea I do not like!"

The young man with him said something in the Letzensteiner German and Julius added, "I think these government inspectors are in trouble down there."

"In danger?" Sir Walter asked, shading his eyes with his hand.

"Oh! In danger of a bath in the river!" said Julius, with a laugh. "Now, Sir Walter and my lady, let me invite you back to my house for luncheon and after it I will show you another route to Marienwald."

The Hawthornes were delighted at this solution. One of the keepers climbed on the box to direct the coachman and the two young gentlemen got into the carriage, which was big enough to hold six. The second was introduced as Anton d'Hautrec, "the husband of my sister Imelda," said the Duke.

It seemed queer to Catherine to be sitting so close to Duke Julius again. He had never taken any interest in her except as the old Grand Duke's granddaughter and proposed heir when he disinherited his son Constant. She had last seen him at the requiem mass in the cathedral when Constant had come so unexpectedly into his own. Julius seemed now to have regained all his old self-confidence; here he was on his own ground, too.

The Varenshalt château was an immense Palladian mansion, standing in well-kept formal gardens. Lady Hawthorne was delighted with its fine rooms and elegant French furniture, all made in the preceding century. Only in the drawing room where they met the ladies of the house were there signs of modern romanticism, draped curtains, small tables and easy chairs.

Julius's younger sister Imelda was dark; his wife, Clara, the Austrian, was fair; both were tall fine-looking women who dressed with style. It was altogether a handsome family; even Imelda's middle-aged father-in-law, Baron d'Hautrec, was a distinguished looking man, with a plump shrewd-eyed face, with whom Sir Walter immediately felt at home.

The talk at first was about the incident at the bridge,

and it was in French, since neither Hautrec nor Duchess Clara understood English.

"This grain registration is an inept idea," said the Baron. "And ineptly carried out."

"By your inefficient successor at the Ministry of the Interior," said Julius, smiling. He added to Sir Walter, "My misguided cousin Constant deprived the Baron of his office last year, in a moment of impatience. We have all been regretting it ever since."

"I understand the whole government was changed then," said Sir Walter.

"Oh, mine was a personal dismissal by the new Grand Duke," said the Baron. "He has a somewhat disreputable cousin whom he insists on protecting from the processes of the law, with which he is too often in conflict."

"Do you mean Rafael le Marre?" asked Sir Walter, interested. "We met him by chance in Trier. He recognized Catherine but I thought him a most undesirable acquaintance for her."

"In Trier? I thought he was in Venice, assisting the revolutionaries there," said Baron d'Hautrec.

"He had just come from there, bringing two of them along with him," said Sir Walter. "One spoke to us—some grey hairs but not older than forty, I should guess. What was his name, my dear?"

"I think it was Caravelli," said Lady Hawthorne, who had an excellent memory for names.

"Luca Caravelli!" said Duchess Clara, suddenly joining in the conversation. She spoke French with a German accent. "Why, he is a wanted man. My uncle—the one who is coming to stay, Julius—was for a time in command of troops in the Veneto and he says these writers are more dangerous than Garibaldi himself, for their works circulate in secret and sow seeds of rebellion. Luca Caravelli writes under the name of Bucintoro, I have heard my uncle say it."

Catherine listened with alarm. It seemed to her most unfortunate that Julius and his friends should have learned of the presence of Rafael's Italian friends in Letzenstein—for she heard Aunt Eleanor saying they were now in Felsenbourg.

"You see!" said young Anton d'Hautrec. "This man le Marre is always in league with foreign revolutionaries. Does not this prove how right my father was to suspect him before? His cousin protects him to his own peril, it seems to me."

"I don't suppose le Marre would be such a fool as to provoke a revolution against Constant," said Julius. "But he uses him as a shield while he does what he pleases, building up his own position among the discontented. I don't trust him; he is a playactor, laughing, and hiding his real aims."

"Luca Caravelli should be handed over to the Austrian authorities," said Clara. "The Grand Duke should not protect rebels, such as he is."

At luncheon the conversation turned to other subjects. One, to Catherine's embarrassment, was herself. Julius was curious to know her English relations' plans for her. He soon discovered that they had only a vague idea of what had happened at the end of Grand Duke Edmond's reign. They thought of Catherine as an English girl, not as a possible heir to the Grand Duchy.

"Catherine is now quite a young lady," said Julius,

smiling at her—a superficial smile. "Have you plans for her marriage?"

"Good gracious, no!" said Aunt Eleanor, falling into English in her surprise. She went on in French, "Catherine is only fourteen. We do not arrange marriages so early, in England."

Julius smiled again. Catherine thought he was pleased; and she was pleased too, if he were to write her off as no danger to his own dynastic ambitions.

After sitting and talking over coffee for some time Julius insisted that they should drive to the abbey in one of his own carriages. His wife came with them but not the Hautrecs.

The great monastery lay in afternoon silence. Although it had been partially burnt and looted during the revolutionary invasion, more than fifty years ago, it had been so well built and restored that it seemed to Catherine to have been there for ever. Inside, the reception rooms, cool and clean, with shuttered windows and plain walls, were restful after the hot August day. The Abbot himself came to welcome them.

Don Hildebrand de Regonal was a tall, solid aristocratic man; it was like meeting another prince, Catherine thought. He did not speak English but had brought with him another monk who had been in England and had written a thesis on the Anglo-Saxon missionary who had founded the monastery over a thousand years before.

"He was a friend of St. Willibrord, who lies buried at Echternach," Dom Winfrid Brenlac told them. He was stocky, with a rosy glistening face, a more plebeian figure than his abbot. He talked to the children and

Miss Lacey while the Abbot entertained the Hawthornes. Dom Winfrid told them how he had travelled about England, visiting cathedrals and reading Anglo-Saxon manuscripts. He had many friends among the Deans and Canons of the Church of England. "Most learned men!" he said with enthusiasm. "And with such love for these dear saints of old Saxon times! But many English people appear not to know that we were converted by their saints."

Giles said, "Lots of them don't know places like this exist! They think the Reformation put an end to monasteries for good."

Presently they were taken to see the picture collection, housed in a long gallery as if in some great house or museum. In fact, as the Abbot explained, most had been given after the Revolution, though some had survived the disastrous fire which had not spread to all parts of the building. They were nearly all religious paintings, dating from the seventeenth century, though with an occasional portrait of an abbot or a pope.

"Our new Archbishop has been visiting us," said Dom Hildebrand. "I think he would have wished us to sell the pictures, if he could have had the money for his own projects! He is an able energetic man, but perhaps *un peu papiste.*"

Sir Walter was surprised. "But surely you are all papists?" he said.

The Abbot laughed gently. "Oh, we all believe the Pope is St. Peter's successor, Christ's Vicar on earth," he said. "But this is different from obeying his every whim. Ah, Sir Walter, your diplomatic career cannot have taken you to Rome!"

Sir Walter had to admit this was true.

Dom Winfrid could scarcely be bothered to tell the children about the pictures; they were all much later than his favourite Anglo-Saxons. Catherine found most of them too large and theatrical; over-dramatization made the Biblical events depicted seem unreal and mythological. For once she agreed with Sir Walter when he remarked in English, "One could do with a Rembrandt, as a relief to all this stylized piety!"

Catherine was most impressed by an early Italian painting of Christ's agony in the garden, which had been presented, as the inscription of the frame stated, by Grand Duchess Marie le Marre, who had died young in 1785. "Rafael's grandmother," she thought.

Next to it, above a marble topped table, was a small drawing of the Colosseum in Rome, an ink and sepia wash which looked modern to Catherine. The others had walked past it but she leaned over the table to look more closely. Among the crowd of figures in the foreground she saw Christ carrying his cross. In Rome, not in Jerusalem.

Then her eye was caught by the signature in the corner. It was a monogram of the capitals R and M, linked by a small l. Catherine had seen it on other drawings.

"Oh!" she cried. "It's by Rafael!"

"We have no Raphaels, Miss Catherine," said Dom Winfred.

"I mean Rafael le Marre," she said blushing.

The Abbot caught the name and turned round. "Yes," he said, in French. "That was given us by a Roman friend. We put it here because Rafael le Marre, though an artist, is the grandson of Grand Duchess Marie. We don't know him. He has never been here. Well! Nowadays it is the fashion to be unbelieving and revolutionary, is it not? The artists and writers, especially, have become infidels."

Catherine thought infidel, unfaithful, was not the right description of Rafael, but she did not dare to argue with the Abbot, especially in French.

They were taken to see the great monastic church, far more beautiful, Catherine thought, than the cathedral in Felsenbourg, because it was uncluttered by later ornament. Presently she heard the Abbot telling Lady Hawthorne that he was responsible for this; he had cleared away all florid additions to "restore the ancient simplicity." He also told them that they were attempting to revive the monastic chant and Catherine was surprised to hear that this had fallen out of use. The monks were learned priests; the laybrothers sturdy farmers. Reviving the medieval offices presented many problems, not all musical, the Abbot said.

Dom Winfrid took the children down to the crypt, his favourite part of the whole abbey because, in its romanesque vaults, he could imagine himself back in Anglo-Saxon days. He showed them the tomb of the saintly missionary St. Willifrid, lamenting that it had been lavishly decorated in modern Gothic style by the Abbot's architects.

"They think nothing is Christian but the middle ages!" he said, with a gesture of despair.

Then they were taken to a parlour and served with wine and coffee and cakes before leaving. Back at the château Julius too tried to press more refreshment on them but the sun was sliding down the sky now, casting long shadows over the formal garden outside, and soon they were all in the big Belgian coach once more and on the road back to Felsenbourg.

The Hawthornes were well content with their day and full of praise for Duke Julius. "Really, he would make a more suitable Grand Duke than Catherine's uncle," said Aunt Eleanor. "His manner is so pleasing."

"He seems to have more political sense too," said Sir Walter.

Giles could see that Catherine was not happy. He added the final teasing remark. "We didn't hear anything very good of your artist friend, did we?"

"Evidently he's a troublesome person," said Sir Walter. "I hope we do not meet him again."

Catherine said nothing, but she felt forlorn. Con was so busy, Yolande so taken up with her baby, and Rafael seemed out of reach. Yet to be in Letzenstein without being with them was more frustrating than being kept in England because there was trouble on the continent. Before they reached the palace Catherine had made up her mind to go by herself and visit the Angel Inn.

4

Image of Conflict

CATHERINE WAS NOT able to put into practice her plan to visit the Angel Inn at once. Saturday was planned for her already and then it was Sunday and she spent a happy time with Con in Yolande's room and witnessed the baby's bath. But on Monday Sir Walter and Lady Hawthorne went to call on the British consul and Miss Lacey went with them. Giles had been invited by Duke Julius to visit the barracks of his regiment.

Con was in his study and when Catherine told him where she wanted to go he said, "Tell Jeanne that Yolande hopes to be able to go down to Xandeln next week." And he sent for Friedel, son of the butler at Xandeln, to go with her. So that was all right.

It was another sunny day and Catherine felt happy as she walked through the narrow streets to St. Michael's Square. Alphonse was standing at the door of the inn. When she asked for Rafael, in French, he replied proudly in English—for it was as a waiter in England that he had met his wife Agnes.

"I don't know if he is in, Miss, but go upstairs please and see for yourself. We keep rooms up there, at the top, for Monsieur Rafael and his friends."

Alphonse knew Friedel and they sat down to talk over tankards of the local beer.

Catherine climbed flight after flight of steep black wooden stairs till she came to the top landing, under a skylight. Through an open door she saw Jeanne standing at a table, ironing a shirt. Jeanne heard her and looked up.

"Oh, it is Cat'erine!" she said in her halting English. She put down the iron and came and kissed Catherine on both cheeks. "I feel I am knowing you, Cat'erine. Raf, he has so much talked of you."

"He talked about you to me," said Catherine shyly.

Jeanne smiled. "Oh! He talks!" she said. "Raf, he is not silent about anyt'ing, not ever."

She took Catherine back into the room. Rafael was not there.

"Where is he now?" Catherine asked.

"He is painting in de . . . *église,* what you call it?" Jeanne said.

"Church," said Catherine. "I can understand French fairly well, you know."

"*Eh, bien,* I will talk in French," said Jeanne, with relief. "Soon I am taking some lunch to them. Paul helps him. Oh! How proud that boy is to be painting alongside Raf!" She wielded her flatiron expertly. "I will just finish this shirt and then we will go. I say to Raf, why is it you get so much dirtier than Luca Caravelli, who contrives sometimes to shave and to wash, even when escaping from the Austrians? Then he says, there was no time. But why is there time for Luca?" She laughed. "Simply he is lazy, is my Rafael."

She hung the clean shirt over the back of a chair, rolled up the ironing cloth and began to collect some things in a basket for lunch. "We shall be early, but then you can see these wall paintings," she said.

Jeanne was wearing a dark green full-skirted dress; she did not put on a hat to go out. They left the inn together and went through the north gate and down through the poor and disreputable part of the town where Catherine had once been lost, towards the riverside wharfs. She told Jeanne about that nightmare flight from the mob on Twelfth Night. "And I daresay I should have frozen to death if Raf had not found me," she said, dramatically.

Jeanne said, "Oh, Raf, he has a great gift for finding people! Sometimes I wonder how we shall fit any more in at Xandeln, big though it is."

They came at last to a building on the wharfside, which Jeanne explained had been converted from an old warehouse by Abbé Félix Thiels, who worked among the dock people, into a church. "He has long been Raf's friend and once he said he wished he had some holy paintings on the walls to brighten things up. So Raf began to paint—years ago, before I knew him. But he never was able to stay long in the country when his uncle was Grand Duke, so the work was always interrupted, sometimes for years. Now he wants to finish it before the Archbishop consecrates the church as he intends to do. Abbé Félix is not sure that the new Archbishop will like Raf's paintings. But it is now too late to alter the scheme."

They went in through a battered heavy door, coming out under scaffolding. Jeanne stood still and looked up. Rafael was sitting on the planks, his legs above their heads. The boy Paul was standing further along; both had paint pots slung round them and brushes in their hands. Rafael looked down.

"Time to eat already?" he said in French and then, seeing Catherine, added in English, "Catherine, good, how nice that you come!"

"She can look at the paintings while you finish," said Jeanne.

"Finish! We don't finish yet," said Rafael. "Never will I paint walls again. This is not my *métier*, I discover, rather too late!"

The old warehouse had a row of horizontal windows high up, in plain glass, so it was quite light. Inside were a few very battered benches. The altar was in an alcove but not against the wall because of the slope of the vault. On it was a small tabernacle for the Sacrament, a crucifix and six stubs of candle stuck in short wooden candlesticks. There was no other decoration in the church but Rafael's paintings, which ran round the whole building.

They were like his drawings, Catherine thought—all people, crowds of people. On each side they were going towards the great Christ on the end wall above the alcove. It was like a medieval Doom, except that this Christ was not enthroned as King and Judge of the world. It was the Christ of the Pavement who sat there, as Pilate's soldiers had dressed him in mockery, with thorns for a crown and blood for his anointing.

Catherine stood gazing up at this figure for some

time in silence. Jeanne stood beside her, looking up too, her face grave.

"It is right," she said softly at last. "Raf has done it right. For when we look at this Christ, we know the wrong we have done."

Then they turned to look at the frieze of figures and Catherine realized that it was like the parable of the sheep and the goats. On the right were people who had loved and cared for others and on the left people who had never troubled themselves about the wretched and hungry. You did not need to be told; you could see it from their faces, expressing in Rafael's bold simple lines their anguish or their greed, their pride or their gentleness.

Toby suddenly bobbed up beside Catherine. "I'm up there," he announced. "He's put me in!" He pointed a small grubby finger and Catherine saw it was true. Among a group of children on the right was a recognizable portrait of Toby.

"Yes, and unfortunately he has put in caricatures of living people in the other side too," remarked Jeanne. "This is what he did some years ago, for some who were powerful under Grand Duke Edmond, sending them to hell like Dante!"

"I am not sending them to hell," called out Rafael from the scaffolding. "They are not yet judged, only coming to judgment. And to show this, Jeanne, I have put some on both sides: the choice is open!"

Jeanne laughed. "Yes! You have become more tolerant, more tender-hearted as you have been longer in this world," she said.

She took Catherine's arm, led her back down the

aisle and pointed up at the last group of hard-faced people in the left wall, with a silent glance, full of meaning. Catherine saw that Rafael had put himself in, as a small figure in the crowd, with his satchel of painting things, kneeling on the ground.

"Are you there?" she whispered to Jeanne.

Jeanne smiled at her. "Well, he wanted to put me on the other wall with the kind sheep," she said. "But I said, I would rather be here with you, among the wild goats! So it's not decided."

Catherine turned to look up at the west wall above the scaffolding. She gasped. Above the doors Rafael was painting a huge St. Michael and Dragon. But the Angel was not, as in the medieval carving, obviously the winner. The Dragon had entwined itself all round him and in fact the Archangel, who was not wearing knight's armour but a long tunic, looked as if he could hardly win.

"Oh, Rafael!" Catherine cried. "The Dragon is winning!"

Rafael laughed. "And don't you think the Dragon thinks he is winning?" he said. "And often he does seem to be winning in this world," he said rather sadly.

Catherine looked to see what Paul was painting. Then she realized that each side of the central figures were angels and saints, smaller, rank on rank up to the ceiling, with gold stars between their haloed heads. Paul was painting the angels' clothes. Rafael was painting the Dragon's snout.

Presently he cleaned off his brush, laid his things aside and climbed down the ladder, Jeanne watching a little anxiously. Paul followed, nimble as a monkey. They all went out into the sunshine. A light breeze was blowing off the river and they went and sat on a convenient pile of timber to eat their lunch. Toby, who was playing outside, ran up when he saw the basket.

Rafael was wearing clothes like the Felsenbourg dockers, old blue trousers, with a long blue blouse belted over them; they were dirty and painty. Paul had on a blouse too and he had tied a handkerchief round his head to keep his straight hair from flopping into his eyes. Now he took it off. Raf's hair was wiry and dark, sticking up rather than down; plaster off the ceiling sprinkled it. Jeanne tried to brush it off with her hand, teasing him about going grey too soon. When Jeanne was there Raf talked mostly in French but sometimes switched to English for Catherine.

"Paul is good at this Michelangelo game," he said. "But I should stick to my crayons and pencils. I am not a painter. Colour I am not good at."

Jeanne was cutting and buttering slices of bread, and handing round pieces of sausage and cheese. There were apples in the basket and Toby seized one at once.

Catherine told Rafael about his picture she had seen at Marienwald and asked, "Why did you put Christ carrying his cross, in Rome?"

"Don't you think he carries it there?" Raf said, in English. "And everywhere in this world."

"Why haven't you been to the Abbey?" asked Catherine. "The Abbot seemed to think you were an infidel, as he called it."

"I have been there," said Rafael, smiling. "But I didn't call on the Abbot! But I saw that old Englishman's tomb, who came to convert us and got knocked on the head for his pains. I hope he feels it was worth it, now that he is in heaven. If he sees how we have turned out, he may wonder!"

But when Catherine told him about the visit to Duke Julius he stopped eating and looked worried. "It is very unlucky, that—their finding out that Luca Caravelli is here," he said.

"*Qu'est ce qu'elle dit?*" Jeanne asked, and so he told her in French.

"Poor Luca! And his little girl has just had this difficult eye-operation," she said. "He and Silvia are at the hospital all day today."

"I hope we can get them to Xandeln soon," said Raf. "I don't trust Baron d'Hautrec not to do some deal with the Austrian police, and hand him over."

"Oh! Was Hautrec there?" Jeanne asked, turning quite pale.

Paul said, "Surely he can't do anything now that he's no longer Minister of the Interior?"

"Well, he can't have Luca arrested," said Rafael. "But he's rather a fellow for working behind the scenes, as you know." But then he added, typically, "*Eh bien!* No use worrying over what hasn't yet happened. Jeanne, you forgot the drink. Paul, go and get us a bottle of *vin ordinaire* from the Ship Inn. Catherine, why don't you go too and see your old friends?"

So Catherine and Paul walked off side by side but shy. Paul had heard more about her adventures than she had about his. Rafael's rare letters had not gone into details. "I brought Paul out of Paris without his English uncle's permission," he had written. "We had a funny time on our travels but in the end his father's will was found and so now he is my legal ward."

Since then Paul had lived over a year with Rafael while Catherine had been living with the Hawthornes in England. Now here they were, both walking along the sunlit wharf to the Ship Inn, where Catherine had been in the snow and Paul in the rain, but both with Raf.

At last Catherine said, "You have an English aunt too, haven't you?"

Paul grinned. "Yes, but not like yours! Your relations are much grander than mine, both here and there." He spoke English well for he had lived some time in Chelsea while his English mother was alive. His father was an artist from Letzenstein, one of Raf's many friends.

"Giles says Con isn't grand *enough* for a Grand Duke," said Catherine.

"Is Giles that boy I saw the day the firecracker went off and we thought Con had been shot?" Paul said. "He looks as if he thought nobody as good as he is."

Catherine thought this so true that she laughed.

They went into the dockside inn and Catherine was greeted with interested cries from the innkeeper's fat wife. As everyone kept saying how much she had grown she was beginning to feel quite grown up. As well as the bottle of wine the woman gave them a bottle of water and some mugs.

"I know Monsieur Rafael," she said. "He will put water in your wine, you children! In his own too, I daresay, to make it go further."

She refused payment. "Only bring those mugs back!"

As they went out they could see Jeanne and Rafael in the distance, leaning over a wall on the quay together, talking. Raf had his hand on her shoulder and they saw him kiss the side of her face, by the ear.

"What did he mean about Baron d'Hautrec working behind the scenes?" Catherine asked.

"Oh, don't you know about the Baron?" said Paul. "No—Raf wouldn't have told you." Then he related how, when Rafael was arrested for kidnapping Paul, the Baron had removed him from the civil jail to the Old Fort, which had been used for political prisoners under Grand Duke Edmond, to question him about his contacts with revolutionaries during the disturbances of January 1848. It was for this illegal act that Constant dismissed Baron d'Hautrec from the post of Minister of the Interior.

"And there he was, pretending Con was shielding Raf from the law!" cried Catherine indignantly. "I'm sure Uncle Walter believed it, too." And then she added, "It does seem unfair that people like the Baron and Duke Julius can appear to have right on their side, when we know they haven't."

"Raf would say the Dragon can dress up as the Angel when he wants to deceive," said Paul. "We've talked about it, while we were painting. What do you think of that, Catherine?"

"I think it's wonderful!" she said with feeling. "How marvelous for you to be able to help with the painting."

Paul grinned with happiness and she knew they would be friends now.

Toby came skipping up as they returned. "Here's the *vino!*" he cried.

Raf turned round and ranged the mugs on the wall. There were only four.

"She's forgotten our youngest child," he said. "Never mind, Toby, you and I will share a mug."

There was almost more water than wine in this one.

"Raf, you spoil it for yourself," Jeanne said. "Have some of mine."

"No, I like it this way," he said. "One can drink more."

He took the mug away from Toby, who seemed likely to finish it. Toby laughed, cut a caper and ran away to the corner among the piles of timber where he was playing.

"He ought to be a clown, that child," said Raf. "But it's bad that he picked up this habit of wanting wine when he was running wild in Venice. He'll lose it when he can drink milk and lemonade at Xandeln."

As they leant on the wall, watching the barges going downstream, a voice behind them cried, "*Raffaele! Ecco un' amico!*"

They all turned round and saw Gaetano coming with his arm across the shoulders of another man, older than himself but younger than Raf, with black hair and dark eyes. Walking with them was a man in a hat, with a sombre face.

"Piero! *Benvenuto!*" cried Rafael. "*Eh! Come sta, amico mio?*"

The black-haired man grasped Raf by both arms and then looked at Jeanne. For a moment he could not speak for emotion.

Jeanne seemed to know him too. "Ah! Piero Biancardi!" she said. "Now you can see that Rafael was not killed in Italy, as you told me in Paris—how long ago? Two years, now?"

Paul said to Catherine, "It must be the man Raf helped to escape from the Austrians that time when he was shot and fell down the mountain, and so injured his back."

Now Piero Biancardi found his voice and began talking to Rafael and Jeanne in a mixture of Italian and French, Gaetano sometimes joining in. The other man stood by in silence till Rafael turned to him, saying in French, "I don't think I know you. Or have I met you with Jacques Roncard, perhaps?"

"Perhaps," the men replied, without much friendliness. "I know Roncard a little."

"This is one who thinks your new Republican party compromises too much," said Gaetano in French, which he spoke fairly well, though with a strong Italian accent. "Armand Grignol, in exile till last year—in Paris."

The conversation became too involved for Catherine to follow. She wandered away, watching the boats on the river, thinking what a lot of queer people Rafael knew. Presently Jeanne came up to her. "Raf says to take you back," she said. "He thinks your uncle and aunt may worry if you have been out too long. And he wants to get on with the painting too."

Gaetano and Grignol were walking away together while Rafael and Piero Biancardi were moving back towards the church, talking hard in Italian. Raf waved to Catherine and Jeanne before he turned in at the door.

As they climbed up the steep narrow streets Jeanne

said, "Sometimes I wish Raf had not got so involved with these Italian republicans. I sympathize with their hopes to free Italy from foreign rule but to so many people in Letzenstein all republicans appear to be violent revolutionaries, and Raf has some powerful enemies here, always waiting to trip him up."

"Why has he?" Catherine asked. It had always puzzled her that Rafael should have enemies; he did not seem to her a dangerous person.

"Men like the Baron judge others by themselves," said Jeanne. "They can't believe that a man in Rafael's position can be without ambition for himself. Do you know, Catherine, it's only in this last year that I've realized that in Letzenstein nobody can forget that Raf is the son of Grand Duke Marius. And you have seen the portraits in the palace—you know that to look at he is almost a caricature of those old le Marre Counts, and of the first who were Grand Dukes."

"But if they think he wants to be Grand Duke, why do they believe he is a revolutionary?" Catherine asked, as they plodded upwards in the afternoon heat.

"I suppose they imagine he wants to make himself a leader through a popular uprising," said Jeanne. "Some kind of little Napoleon! How very unlike Raf—but these men in office or in the army command don't know him, only their idea of him." After a moment she added, "I know he's a puzzle to these republicans of Roncard's too. He doesn't see why Con should not be a constitutional ruler and Letzenstein go on being a Grand Duchy. I didn't like the look of that Grignol, did you? He seemed a fanatic to me. Well! Soon we shall be back at Xandeln. Things are simpler there."

Catherine was pleased that Jeanne should confide in her. Ever since she had seen Rafael's sketch of Jeanne she had been fascinated by her, interested that she should have made a name for herself dancing in the theatre and then given it all up, when she thought Raf was dead, to nurse poor people in Paris. And now this independent person somehow managed to be married to Rafael and to join in his life, complicated as it was by so many problems not of his own making.

When they reached the Angel Inn, she was not pleased to see Sir Walter and Giles sitting outside it, waiting for her. It meant she had to say goodbye to Jeanne at once and go home with them.

Uncle Walter could not be angry with Catherine since Con had given her permission and had sent Friedel with her. But he was annoyed with Con. "He has no business to let you go off to spend the day with those people," he said. "I shall have to speak to him about it."

Giles began to talk about Duke Julius and his Hussars. "You know, the Letzenstein army may be small, but it's always been well-trained. They've fought in a lot of historic battles. Apparently it was worthwhile having them on one's side in the old days. Napoleon rather demoralized them, Duke Julius said. He is trying to build up their reputation again."

Catherine was glad Giles felt more respect for Letzenstein, though she wished he had not chosen Julius Varenshalt as his hero and guide to its history and politics.

At dinner Sir Walter began to complain, of course politely, of Catherine's being allowed to visit Rafael and Jeanne le Marre. But, as he put it later, he came up against a brick wall.

"My cousin may be eccentric," said Con. "But I would trust him with anyone I loved, at any time."

In fact, Con was so annoyed at Sir Walter's attitude that the next evening, after dinner, he took Catherine with him to the Angel. It was growing dark as they walked through the streets, but still warm. Con had put on an old smoking jacket and went hatless, his thick dark hair, which had some grey hairs in it now, sticking up in tufts as usual. Miss Lacey had once said he looked "rough" for a prince; certainly he was big and bony, with a knobbly, craggy face, but for all his height and size he was not clumsy. Catherine had once watched him escaping from enemies over snow-covered roofs, surefooted and agile. She often felt that being a Grand Duke was not what he was made for. He would have made a good pioneer and explorer.

They heard music as they came into St. Michael's Square and saw some young people dancing a folk dance in the corner by the Angel inn. Raf was sitting on one of the benches by the wall, with his feet up on a chair, playing an accordion for them. Toby was jigging out a dance of his own beside him and Jeanne was sewing a button on Paul's shirt as he sat there facing her.

When Rafael saw them he ended the interminable folk tune with a long drawn chord, resisting the young people's demands for more. Con and Catherine sat down opposite and Agnes came out with a bottle of wine "on the house" she said.

"No wonder Alphonse didn't make out with an inn

before," Con said in English. "No, really, Agnes, I am going to pay! Don't tell Alphonse if it will cause a scene."

Agnes laughed and slipped the money into her pocket.

Presently Con began to talk to Rafael about Luca Caravelli. "I didn't realize he was wanted by the Austrian police," he said. "Is he really a friend of yours, Raf, or just someone you have befriended?"

"No, a good friend," Raf said. "I knew him first in Rome, then I met them both in Milan when Silvia was singing there. I went to England to see Luca. Yes! My London visit, when I learned my perfect English!" He smiled at Catherine. "As for the Austrian police, they want practically everyone in Italy. Even they wanted me, you know that, Con."

"Raf, be serious," said Con. "Julius was serious enough today when he came to see me about it. I think your friend had better go on to England at once."

"Poor Luca!" said Rafael. "His little girl has just had this eye-operation yesterday. She has to lie still in the dark. All day Luca and Silvia are at the hospital. No, he cannot leave yet, Con."

Con frowned, fiddling with his glass.

"Here is Silvia," said Jeanne. Silvia and Gaetano came towards them across the square, Gaetano with his jacket slung over one shoulder like a bullfighter's cloak. The conversation became French and Italian; it seemed that Silvia and Luca were now taking turns at the hospital. Nobody introduced Con and Catherine had a feeling that Silvia did not know who he was. She was in good spirits, for Chiara had come through the operation well and they hoped for a good result. Raf was gently playing a little tune on his accordion, a lullaby, and Silvia began to sing softly.

"Oh, Silvia, do sing for us!" begged Paul, and the others added their pleas.

Silvia was a singer by profession; she had met Jeanne in their theatre days. She looked across at Rafael and said something in rapid Italian, laughing.

"Scorning my old squeeze-box," he said "Says she won't sing to that!"

Silvia reverted to French. "But Raf, in Italy you used to play the guitar."

"And he does now," Jeanne said. "But it's at Xandeln."

"I daresay Alphonse has one around," said Rafael. "Go and see, Paul."

Paul jumped up and ran indoors; he soon came out again with a guitar. But Gaetano took it from him. "It's for Raf," Paul said, unwilling to yield it.

"Oh! Gaetano plays much better than I do," said Raf.

When Silvia sang, in her clear soprano, people in the square stopped to listen. She sang some dramatic Italian songs and Gaetano, with his foot on a stool, accompanied her on the guitar. There was even applause after one song and Silvia, suddenly aware of the audience, would sing no more.

"So! Now we all sing!" Raf said, starting up on the accordion with a ballad they all seemed to know, except Catherine. But she did not mind; indeed she was soon able to hum the tune, though she could not always catch the words. She was happy to sit there listening, leaning back in her chair so that she could see, far above the steep roofs, pinpoints of stars in the summer night sky.

When Con took her home, some time later, they were still singing outside the Angel Inn, and the young people were once more dancing to the endless old tunes.

5

Actual Conflict

ON THE WEDNESDAY of that week Miss Lacey and Catherine went out to buy a christening present for the baby, for he was to be baptized on Saturday, August 25th, that being the feast of St. Louis, his patron saint. It was another dry day which promised to be hot later, so they started about ten. Catherine was to be godmother to Christian Louis and wanted to get him a silver spoon and fork in a case. The silversmiths were in a street which ran into St. Michael's Square and as they came out of the shop Catherine saw Paul hurrying by, with a very anxious face.

"Paul! What's the matter?" she called out.

"I can't stop, I must find Raf," he answered. "I hope he hasn't gone down to the church yet. Trouble with Gaetano."

Catherine immediately went after him, Miss Lacey following with faint protests.

The morning sunlight slanted across the front of the Angel inn. Rafael, in the workman's overalls he used for painting the murals, was standing outside, leaning on his stick, talking to Piero Biancardi in Italian.

Paul ran up to him. "Raf! Gaetano's gone to the Republican meeting."

"How, gone? I told him this must not be," Rafael said, annoyed. "Luca promised they would not take part, after he heard what Con had said."

"I don't suppose Luca knows," said Paul. "But I've just seen Gaetano with Armand Grignol and some students on their way to Palace Square—with a red flag, too."

"*Peste!*" said Rafael, crossly. He explained to Piero in Italian and then said to Paul, "Run upstairs and tell Jeanne I've gone to keep an eye on Gaetano—to bring him back, if possible."

"Oh, Raf, but I want to come with you!"

"No. It's not a meeting for children."

"I'm fifteen!" cried Paul indignantly. "Besides, Raf, I could run messages for you."

"True enough," said Rafael. He turned to Catherine and said in English, "Catherine, *chérie*, would you then tell Jeanne, please?" Then he smiled at her and added, "What a pretty hat! I think I'll take mine, as it is so sunny." He picked up his big hat from a table and put it on the back of his head, setting off at once with Piero and Paul.

Catherine went into the inn before Miss Lacey could object and climbed up to the top of the house. She could hear Jeanne singing one of her favourite old ballads. She had an alto voice and sang in a straightforward way. She was making the beds as she sang, punching the pillows. When Catherine appeared and said in French that Rafael had gone to the republican meeting—she did not know what the term was in

French and had to call it a "rendez-vous"—to fetch Gaetano back, Jeanne was surprised.

"Will there be trouble?" she said, rather anxiously. "I think I will go to see what is happening. Oh—*bonjour*, Miss Lacey."

Miss Lacey had just reached the top of the stairs only to find they were about to descend. Jeanne took pity on her and asked her into the sitting room for a cup of coffee.

She had made the three attics of the inn into a temporary home, not only for herself and Rafael but for Luca and Silvia too. Gaetano had a bed in an alcove on the landing and Paul and Toby slept on mattresses in the sitting room.

"It's all right in summer, because we can stay outside till late," said Jeanne. "And eat dinner in the inn."

Catherine was interested to see how they all fitted in and Miss Lacey was relieved to find that Jeanne was evidently a good housewife.

Presently they went down and walked along the streets together towards the Palace Square, where the meeting was being held outside the Chamber of Deputies, shut now for the vacation. By the time they reached the square it was past eleven and the meeting was in full swing, orators speaking from the steps of the fountain in the middle. It was a crowd of men; hardly any women were about.

It was quite impossible to get across to the palace. Miss Lacey was alarmed but Jeanne said, "I expect it will be over by dinnertime. Let's go over to the Belmont Hotel. We can watch from there and go inside if there's trouble."

As they went round to the hotel, the best in Felsenbourg, Jeanne told Catherine how she had come there from Valmay with Con in March 1848, to rescue Raf from the Old Fort. "Con has shut that place now," she said. "He disbanded the special corps of police and sacked the Baron and Colonel Stenken, who was the commandant, under the old Grand Duke. But I believe Duke Julius took Stenken into his regiment afterwards."

They stood on the pavement outside the hotel. Jeanne shaded her eyes, searching the crowd of men for Rafael.

But it was Gaetano they saw first. He had climbed on to the steps of the fountain, a noticeable figure in his white shirt, with a knotted red neckerchief, and he was shouting in his Italianate French. He had a strong clear voice and Jeanne could hear quite a lot.

"Oh dear," she presently said. "It seems there's an Austrian general calling on Con—staying with Julius Varenshalt, he says. Gaetano, of course, wants to make a demonstration against him."

"There's Paul," said Catherine, catching sight of Paul's blue shirt and light brown hair, on a lower level than all the men's heads. "Now I can see Raf too. They're trying to get nearer to the fountain—to the right of it."

"Ah! I see them, " Jeanne said. "I expect Raf wants to stop that silly boy making inflammatory speeches."

Miss Lacey, who was peering through her lorgnette, said nervously, "Isn't that Duke Julius's carriage, coming into the square on the left?"

It certainly was the Varenshalt closed carriage which

drove into the square, with the Duke, his wife Clara and her Austrian uncle sitting plain to view behind the glass windows.

Gaetano gave a howl of rage at the sight and rushed down from the fountain, followed by a lot of other young men, equally excited. They began to hurl big stones at the carriage. They were cobble stones, which they must have prized up already.

Jeanne bit her lip and groaned. "Oh, what's going to happen now? Look, there are the Civil Guards! Oh, fool, fool of a boy!"

The horses of the carriage plunged about in fright; the glass of one of its windows was smashed to bits. They could see Julius pushing his wife down on the seat, below window level. Then he shouted to the Civil Guards out of the other side. In another moment a fight between the guards and the young demonstrators was going on round the carriage.

"Catherine! There's Sir Walter, just come out of the palace," said Miss Lacey. "Giles too."

Duke Julius jumped out of the further side of the carriage and seized a pistol from a Civil Guard. Standing on the step he fired over the roof, and hit one of the demonstrators, not Gaetano.

Instantly a great roar went up from the Republicans, who surged forward. None were armed and when the guards began to fire, they fell back. Several were wounded. It was agonizing watching it all. Catherine found she was holding her breath till it hurt. She was trying to see where Rafael and Paul were, but Raf's dark blouse was not easy to pick out. Then she saw his hat, his big black hat, which had slipped behind his head, hanging by its strings. He was still trying to get to Gaetano, who was in the forefront of the scrum, laying about him with a truncheon he had seized from a Civil Guard.

"Oh! They've got Gaetano! They've handcuffed him!" Catherine cried. "He's arrested!"

"*Mon dieu, quel malheur!*" moaned Jeanne.

There was such a scuffle and struggle going on that it was difficult to see what was happening but when Gaetano was dragged behind the carriage by the guards who had captured him—he was still trying to fight back—they all saw Rafael get free of the crowd and dive after him. They saw him using his stick as a weapon; he hit first one guard and then the other on the wrists with such force and precision that they dropped Gaetano's arms. Piero, who was close behind, seized hold of Gaetano and rushed him off, handcuffs and all, while Rafael backed after them, using his stick as if it were a sword.

"Fencing!" said Jeanne, with a gasp that was half a sob and half a laugh. "Raf, he used to be so good at fencing!"

They never expected Rafael to get away but in fact the Civil Guards had their work cut out to deal with the demonstrators. Piero pulled Gaetano back into the crowd of Republicans.

Catherine saw Paul dodging about, trying to help Rafael. Then her attention was distracted by the sight of Con coming down the steps from the palace, almost two at a time. He made for the beleaguered carriage but before he reached it a contingent of Varenshalt's Hussars rode into the square with drawn sabres.

It was the end of the demonstration. The young men fled before the charging horses. In the ensuing scrimmage Jeanne rushed away from the hotel, pushing her way towards Rafael and Paul. Catherine saw them all swept down a side street and she was left with Miss Lacey as the square emptied before their eyes.

Then she saw Giles, on the palace steps, pointing at them. He had seen them and next moment he and his father were coming across to the hotel.

"Catherine! Thank God you are safe!" cried Sir Walter, red in the face with heat and alarm. "What a terrible affair! And it all happened so suddenly."

"We saw the whole thing!" cried Giles excitedly. "Wasn't the Duke brave? We saw your revolutionary artist friend too, fighting the police."

Catherine's knees were trembling. She felt suddenly dizzy. They took her into the Hotel Belmont and made her sit down. Smelling salts, glasses of water, brandy, were thrust upon her and presently she felt better. "I suppose that's what it's like fainting, nearly," she thought, interested to know.

Then Miss Lacey took her arm and they walked back across the square to the palace. In the entrance hall Con was talking in German to the Austrian general, who was purple in the face from this unexpected violent interlude on his holiday, and to Julius, who appeared to be urging some course of action with impatience.

"What was Duke Julius saying?" Catherine asked Miss Lacey, as they went upstairs.

Miss Lacey had learned German and was well up in

it at present because she was translating a book on Pond Life by her friend Professor Schwartzdorf, now of Felsenbourg University, once Con's tutor.

"I think he's saying that the Prince—the Grand Duke I mean—ought to declare a state of emergency and rule by martial law," she said, "The Duke thinks it's the only way to rid the country of these dangerous revolutionaries."

"And Con was saying no?" Catherine asked. "He looked as if he was."

"Yes, he said he thought everything would calm down in a day or two," said Miss Lacey. "I hope he's right."

Catherine was sent to rest after luncheon, but by then she had quite recovered and found it intolerable to lie on her bed, not knowing what had happened to Rafael and his friends. So presently she got up and put on her dress and shoes and went out into the passage. It was silent and empty except for a fly buzzing against a shut window. It was warm and stuffy indoors.

Catherine went downstairs, right down to the ground floor and across the chequered pavement of the gallery where the old Grand Duke had once called Rafael a traitor, and out on to the terrace. The heat struck her like a furnace blast, rebounding from the stone paving. She went along to the end and down the steps to the stable yard arch. She had never seen it except under snow; now there were lavender bushes with bees among them, each side of the steps.

No one was in the yard either. Catherine walked across its cobbled space under the further archway and out into the street at the back. This was the way the cart had come which had brought Rafael a prisoner to the palace in the near-revolution of January 1848. "Time passing . . . how mysterious it is," she thought. "Where is it now—what happened then?"

By now Catherine knew the way from the palace to St. Michael's Square very well. It was not far away; nothing was far in Felsenbourg. She would hardly get lost anywhere in it now. She heard a clock strike two quarters: half past two. After the excitements of the morning the city seemed to have gone to sleep just as usual. It was not such a long siesta as southern countries took but it was somewhat vague in extent. Shops seemed to open again when they felt like it and did more business in the evening than in the afternoon.

St Michael's Square was empty except for a few pigeons picking about and an old beggar asleep on the sunny steps of the church. And in front of the Angel inn Rafael was sitting alone at a table with a plate in front of him—alone, except for Toby, who was as usual standing at his elbow and helping himself to bits of the belated dinner which Rafael did not seem very interested in.

Catherine went quickly across the cobbles. "Oh, Raf! You are all right? You got away!"

He looked up and smiled but she saw he was glancing over her shoulder. "Anyone with you, Catherine?"

She shook her head. "I slipped out by myself," she said. "I just had to know what had happened to you." She sat down at the table, the other side from Toby. "What about Gaetano?"

"They're all safe, they've all gone," Rafael said. "I've only just got back from seeing them off. I sent Paul to fetch Luca from the hospital. He hadn't even heard of the row and I had a job persuading him to go. Gaetano had to go in his handcuffs! There wasn't time to get them off."

He leant his head on his hand and Catherine realized that he was very tired, too tired to eat. Toby picked up a carrot, dusted with parsley. "May I have this, Raf?"

"Of course have it, little donkey!" said Raf, smiling. "Have what you like—I want it not."

"Where have they gone?" Catherine asked.

"*Caterina mia*, the fewer people know that the better," said Rafael. "Out of Felsenbourg, that is enough."

"Silvia too?"

"No, no, she stays because of Chiara. Jeanne will help her. They will be allowed to bring the child home, tomorrow or the next day. She is all right but has to be kept quiet and in the dark—that's hard at five years old."

"Tie her down," suggested Toby.

"What a brigand you are, Toby!" said Raf. He tapped the little boy on the chest. "What have you in here instead of a heart?"

Toby looked very knowing. "A clock, perhaps?" he said.

Catherine and Rafael were both laughing when a shadow fell across the table. They looked up and saw Con standing there. He was looking grave, almost grim. He did not sit down but stood there, towering over them.

"Rafael," he said at last, "how could you do that?"

Raf seemed surprised. "Do what?" he said. "What's

the matter, Con? You look as if someone had been killed, but nobody has, so far as I know."

"Don't laugh about it," said Con, with deep indignation. "You, Raf, to join with those wild students in attacking a foreign visitor, with Julius's wife in the carriage too—how could you do that? And that young Italian rabble rouser—surely you could have prevented his taking part? Now we have the most difficult situation on our hands—the Republicans enraged at being fired on, the Austrian general demanding Caravelli as the cause of it all, and Julius pressing for martial law. And you can only laugh!"

Rafael was certainly not laughing by the time he had finished. "That's how it appears to you, Con?" he said slowly, gazing up at his tall cousin with those very keen blue eyes of his. "That I was responsible for what happened this morning?"

"I saw you myself, hitting the Civil Guards with your stick—and not gently," Con said.

"Better a Civil Guard with a bruised wrist than Gaetano a problem prisoner," said Raf.

Con struck the table with his fist so hard that the plate jumped. Catherine had never seen him so angry before.

"Raf! I would never have thought you could do this!" he said. "Well! You must take the consequences, that's all. I can't do anything about it. Indeed, I have no desire to help you escape the consequences of such lawless irresponsible acts." He turned suddenly to Catherine and said shortly, "Catherine, come with me please."

She stood up, nervously glancing from one to the other.

"Con, listen—" Raf began, but Con would not listen.

"I can't see how I can listen to you ever again," he said, and Catherine realized that he was not only angry but miserable. "Only the other day I said I would trust you with anyone. Now—this! You care more for your Italian revolutionary friends than you do for us here, that's plain. No! This is altogether too much, Raf. I will not listen to any excuses. I do not see how I can trust you, now."

He took Catherine's hand and abruptly walked off. Looking back over her shoulder Catherine saw Rafael sitting hunched up over the table, his chin on his fists. He looked, if possible, even more unhappy than Con.

Con strode through the square and into the silversmiths' street, where the shutters were coming down and people beginning to move about again. He was so silent and grim that Catherine dared say nothing.

But presently he spoke to her. "How was it you were there, Catherine?"

"I went to see—to see if they were all right," Catherine faltered.

"He didn't send for you?"

"Oh no," said Catherine. She plucked up her courage and went on, "Please, Con, Rafael told Gaetano not to go to that meeting. And Luca wasn't there at all. He was at the hospital."

Con stopped. "What? Why did he go himself, then?"

"He went to try to get Gaetano to come back," said Catherine. "That's what he was doing all the time. I was with Jeanne, we followed them. He didn't attack the carriage, Con, he didn't." Her courage returned as she spoke. "He only hit those guards to get Gaetano away."

"Catherine! You saw all this? But Julius said—"

"Oh! she cried. "You know how Julius hates Raf! He always believes the worst of him, he always suspects him of being a rebel, you know he does. But we were there, Con, before you came out—we saw it all. Gaetano made a speech and those young men went after him to attack the carriage. It wasn't the Republicans who made the trouble, it was Gaetano and the students. It was only when Julius fired at them that the Republicans began to fight too."

She looked up at Con's face and saw the lines in it relax. "Why didn't he tell me?" he said at last. "Raf! Why didn't he explain?"

With daring Catherine said, "You didn't give him much chance."

Con smiled. "I suppose not," he said. "It seemed so inexplicably dreadful to think of Raf doing something like that. Come! Let's go back now and make him an apology."

Catherine almost skipped as they started back to the square. She could not bear two people she liked so much to quarrel.

There were more people about now and a cart loaded with vegetables was trundling across the square so that until they passed it they did not see the scene outside the Angel.

Then Catherine cried, "Oh, Con! He's arrested again!"

Two Civil Guards were just in the act of fastening handcuffs on Rafael, who was now standing up. Toby was hammering one of the guards with his fists, but the man took no more notice than if he had been a fly. Toby was crying and shouting and Raf was trying to quiet him.

"Toby, cry not—nothing terrible happens. Soon I come back. Go, find Jeanne, Toby."

Then he saw Catherine and Con and became silent, the unhappy expression returning to his face.

Con strode up to the table and the Civil Guards, surprised at this sudden arrival of their Grand Duke, let go of Rafael and saluted so smartly that he nearly lost his balance and grabbed one of them by the shoulder.

For a moment no one knew what to say. Then Con addressed the guards in French, asking what they were doing.

The senior guard saluted again. "We're just rounding up the known rioters, sir," he replied. "Orders from headquarters."

Con hesitated, uncertain what he ought to do. Rafael said, in English, "Why did you come back, Con?"

"To apologize," said Con. "Catherine explained what happened. I am sorry, Raf. I should have known you better."

Rafael's face looked quite different as he said, "Thank you, Catherine!"

"It did look bad against you, Raf," said Con, defending himself.

Raf smiled. "All right! It is all right, Con. I suppose it did look to you as if I had joined the stone-throwers!"

Con seized both his hands, ignoring the handcuffs, and shook them warmly.

The two Civil Guards stood like stuffed dummies but for days afterwards they were to entertain their friends with accounts of the scene: the Grand Duke shaking hands with his cousin (whom they knew all about) just after he had been arrested for riotous and revolutionary behaviour.

Jeanne came hurrying out of the inn, asking what was happening.

Rafael answered her, in French of course, "Just another little spell in gaol, Jeanne my dear. Don't worry! Hitting Civil Guards is not a capital crime, is it sergeant?"

The Civil Guard barely suppressed a grin.

Jeanne turned to Con with an anxious look. "He can't do anything," Raf said quickly. "He's a law-abiding Grand Duke and I, strange to say, am a law-abiding rioter."

The sergeant looked at Con who said, "I suppose you must take him now, for the time being." To Jeanne he added, "We will get him a good lawyer. There can be no serious charge and now there's no Old Fort, you know—no Baron d'Hautrec waiting in the wings to deal out illegal penalties."

Jeanne smiled, but still anxiously.

"Come, give me a kiss and cheer up," said Raf. Ever since Con's apology he seemed in very good spirits and he went off now quite jauntily, though his uneven gait was more noticeable than it had been before the violent activities of the morning.

Toby ran after him and had to be fetched back by Jeanne. Then he began to howl. "Let me go too! I want to go with Raf," he cried.

Jeanne sat down and held him, struggling, on her knee, and hugged him.

"Poor Toby!" she said to them. "Raf takes the place of his lost father. He can't bear to let him out of his sight. Toby," she said, trying to speak to him in English, "soon we go to see Raf in his prison, you and me."

The little boy quieted down gradually, leaning his head against Jeanne's breast and sucking his thumb like a much younger child.

Con sat down and told Jeanne of his misunderstanding with Rafael, and he apologized all over again to her. Evidently it still worried him.

"Oh! Raf does not mind now, I can tell from his face," she said. "He will be gay, in prison! But he may tease you about it later, I fear."

"Things are so very difficult just now," said Con, with a sigh. "It seemed the last straw to have Raf turn unreliable. Well! Soon we shall be at Xandeln, Jeanne. I want to send Yolande and the baby as soon as possible after the christening. Can you go with them?"

Jeanne glanced at him, colouring a little. "How long will he, will Rafael be in gaol, please?"

"Oh, I expect they will all be in court before the end of the week," said Con. "I hope we can get them off with fines. The Austrian leaves Julius's house tomorrow, so he won't feel insulted if no one is shot for throwing stones at him." He got up. "But I am afraid it will be humiliating for Rafael, tried along with a bunch of boys, and he now well over thirty!"

Jeanne smiled and said, "I don't think he will mind that. He would only have minded if you had been thinking what others may think—that he was really taking part in that senseless act of violence."

"It was stupid of me not to realize there must be some other explanation," said Con, as he got up to leave. "Because as long as I've known him—since we grew up, anyway—he has never fought to attack, only to defend."

"Not before you grew up?" Catherine asked.

Con laughed. "When we were boys he attacked me sometimes," he said. "If he couldn't make me agree to do what he wanted!"

Jeanne wanted to hear this in French and when she did it amused her very much. "I know this in Raf," she said. "His determination to get one to assent to his will! Just so he would make me to marry him . . . and he won in the end."

As they walked home Con said to Catherine, "Jeanne is a person I admire very much. It is wonderful that Raf has found someone like her. Being married to him must be like living in the path of hurricanes!"

6

Trials and Ceremonies

THE RIOTERS WERE brought before the court on Friday, which was August 24th. Because he was Grand Duke, Constant himself could not attend, but he allowed Catherine to go and sit in the gallery with Miss Lacey. Sir Walter Hawthorne was doubtful of the wisdom of this, fearing that Her Majesty's government might somehow become involved in diplomatic exchanges; but as Felsenbourg seemed quiet now, at any rate on the surface, he did not object and even allowed Giles to go with them, thinking it part of his education to see how a foreign court was conducted.

The lawyers and the judge wore different costumes from the English ones and the children found it hard to believe in a judge who did not wear a long curled wig. But his face under his official cap, Catherine observed, was legal-looking. The proceedings were in French, so they could follow most of what went on.

There were about a dozen prisoners, all very young except for Rafael, as Con had expected. They looked quite respectable, for their parents had taken their best clothes to the prison and they sat like students waiting for a lecture. Rafael was odd man out, for though

Jeanne had taken him a clean white shirt he was wearing the only clothes he had in Felsenbourg, besides his painting overalls—the worn black suit in which he had lived through the siege of Venice and escaped across Europe.

It turned out that none of the students was a member of the Republican Party, and this was a point not only in their favour but in the Party's. Its leader, Jacques Roncard, was in the gallery and he relaxed when this became clear and began talking to his neighbour. To Catherine he looked just like any other politician. He had grey hair and a big nose.

Rafael was the only one whose case took longer than a few minutes to review. The prosecutor seemed to be bringing up a lot of past history against him. Paul, sitting with Jeanne just behind Catherine, leant over and whispered, "Someone has tried to make out a real case against Raf."

"Julius?" she hazarded.

"Probably behind it," said Paul. "But I bet it was put together by Baron d'Hautrec. Only he could know so much about Raf's activities."

When the prosecution speech was finished Catherine felt quite anxious. A picture seemed to have been built up of a scheming person who was not a member of the new Republican party only because he had been involved much longer in revolutionary conspiracy.

Giles said, "He's certainly been mixed up in a lot of political incidents."

"Incidents happen to him," said Paul at once. "He doesn't start them."

Con had engaged a very good counsel to defend

Rafael. What he did was to make it clear that most of the prosecution case was irrelevant to the present charge. Rafael was charged with attacking the Civil Guard, and that was all. Nobody could even prove that he had taken part in the attack on the Duke's carriage. All that could be established was his rescue of his young Italian friend from the police. And this, the lawyer pointed out, though reprehensible, was not a serious crime. He refused to be side-tracked into political argument or go into the question of the young Italian's identity and present whereabouts.

Catherine heard some people near her talking in low voices. "This would have gone very differently in the old Grand Duke's day," said one. "It would have been a political trial and le Marre would probably have ended up in the Rotberg fortress for life."

"Well, thank God we've moved on from there," said the other.

The students were let off with fines; Rafael with a bigger fine. The judge gave them a stern lecture on the evils of lawless violence and devoted his best efforts to Rafael's case. Technically he was only guilty of assaulting the officers of law and order, so he was only to be fined. But really, the judge said, he was far more guilty than the students because at his age and with his family connexions, he ought to know better. He hoped that Rafael le Marre would take warning and live a more respectable life in the future.

Catherine could hear Paul muttering with indignation at this moral lecture of his guardian, but Rafael himself did not appear at all concerned. He listened with an expression of detached interest, as if the judge were talking of somebody else. Catherine could see that this annoyed the judge, who grew more stern as he proceeded.

But at last even the judge had said his say and the court was dismissed. Rafael's fine was paid for him; by Con, Catherine supposed. They all went downstairs and saw him in the hall surrounded by the students and their families. Far from taking any notice of the judge, they all seemed to be congratulating Rafael and some were shaking hands with him.

"You seem to have made friends with those boys," said Jeanne, when they eventually got near him.

"*Eh bien*! We have had two nights and one day of non-stop talking, in gaol!" said Rafael, with a laugh. "A political marathon! And I was hoping to sleep!"

"Talking about what?" Catherine asked.

"Oh, the difference between autocratic rulers—not always monarchs, Napoleon providing an example,—and the constitutional kind, with a Chamber of Deputies, like Constant," said Raf. "And how Republics are sometimes, but not always, the answer to problems, while violent revolutions rarely, if ever, produce improvements for the people, generally setting up a new governing class not held in check by traditional customs."

Then he added, with a laugh, "That is *my* version! But it emerged through hours of arguments, believe me!"

As they went out of the Palais de Justice he stopped to speak to a Civil Guard on duty, in the German dialect. It seemed a friendly conversation and as they moved on Catherine asked, "What were you saying to him?"

"Oh, that's one of the poor fellows I hit so hard with my stick," said Raf cheerfully. "I was apologizing to him. I said I would much rather have hit Gaetano, the silly young fool, but I had to get him away or it would have made trouble for someone worth six of him. Of course the guard knew I meant Luca, they've all been told to look for him. But I don't think they are looking very hard! You see, in Letzenstein we are sympathetic to nations that want their independence because we have always had difficulty in keeping ours, with France on one side and the Germanies on the other."

Paul had glanced round at the Guard. "He looks very friendly considering how hard you hit him!"

Rafael laughed. "Oh well! I don't suppose he gets apologies from all the fellows who hit him!" he said.

Miss Lacey, with Catherine and Giles, now left the others to return to the palace, just across the square. Giles looked preoccupied. Presently he said, "I don't believe the judge's remarks made any impression on him at all."

Catherine laughed. "Why should they? The judge didn't know what he was talking about."

"Oh, didn't he?" said Giles. "Well, it's plain enough that Rafael has been influencing those students in gaol—"

"Giles!" Catherine interrupted him, "But he was influencing them to moderate views—you heard what he said just now."

"What he said to *you*," said Giles. "But he knows that Luca Caravelli is wanted by the Austrian authorities—I bet he knows where he is, too. He's just as much mixed up with rebels and Revolutionaries as he was in 1848."

"But Giles, surely you don't think Raf is a dangerous revolutionary conspirator, or ever was?" Catherine said, exasperated.

"I don't know about dangerous," said Giles, "but he's obviously against law and order. He didn't care tuppence for that court or anything that was said. He knew he was going to get off. I suppose your precious uncle paid the bill. I think he's a fool to trust that cousin of his, so much cleverer than he is. He manipulates Constant for his own ends."

Catherine was so angry she could say nothing at all.

That same Friday members of the principal families of Letzenstein and Valmay were arriving for the christening, headed by Yolande's aunt, the Duchesse de Noisaud, whose husband was Minister for Valmay since the recent union of the two small states. Christian Louis would inherit both through his parents. Until they reached Felsenbourg they were unaware that their great-nephew's godfather had just been taken to court for a breach of the peace. They were shocked to discover that Constant had not altered his arrangements in view of this, and Catherine heard many criticisms of her uncle's weakness with respect to his scapegrace cousin. They all seemed to know Rafael, but from a distance only; several remarked how disreputable he always looked.

Con refused to be moved. "We shall have the mass at St. Michael's in the morning, for the re-opening of the church," he said. "Rafael will have to be there, as a knight of the Order, and as he will look like all the rest of us, nobody will think he has just come out of gaol."

Yolande remarked that she could not imagine how Rafael would manage to look like all the other knights of St. Michael but she laughed when Con said, "At any rate his clothes for it are here, so he won't turn up at the christening in that ancient black suit, which looks as if it will fall to bits before he gets back to Xandeln."

Some other visitors arrived in Felsenbourg on Friday, the Altenbergs of Nordwick, Con's cousins on his mother's side and his allies from boyhood. In the afternoon he asked Giles if he would like to come with Catherine and meet them. "Edward d'Altenberg is about your age," he said.

"Edward is exactly one month older than me," said Catherine. "So we are both a bit older than Giles." She liked to insist on her few months' seniority to Giles because he always behaved as if he were the elder.

Giles came. He had heard about the Altenbergs from Catherine, how they were all half-English and that Duke Gabriel bred racehorses at Nordwick. Edward, Gabriel's nephew, the son of his brother Gilbert, was at school in England, but at Winchester, not at Eton. Catherine had seen him in London recently, but Giles had been away at the time and had not met him.

The Altenbergs had a big old house, standing in its

own garden, next to the park in the southern suburb of Felsenbourg, outside the walls. Catherine had only seen it in winter, when the long pond in the park was frozen, where she had caught sight of Con skating in his trapper's coat and had been impressed by his high speed jumping turns—Con just back from Canada where he had spent several years, exiled by his father. Now the pond, or lake, as it was more grandly called, was covered in little rowing boats and the park was full of afternoon strollers. A band was playing on the bandstand, surrounded by beds of scarlet geraniums, and people sitting on the green park chairs applauded in a casual way between the numbers.

Con drove himself; they sat beside him in a light trap. Catherine knew he liked to drive himself when he could, but Giles was surprised to go out with the Grand Duke in such an informal way.

"Oh! the griffins!" said Catherine, as they drove between stone posts crowned with figures of these heraldic beasts, on the further side of the park. "The griffin is the Altenberg crest," she explained to Giles. "Rafael's is the phoenix."

"How can he have a crest?" Giles asked, in a scornful tone.

"Why, because he is le Marre of Xandeln—the last le Marre," Con answered him. "His mother's being a commoner does not deprive him of his name, Giles. Some people think it should not have deprived him of the Duchy. He is in fact Count of Xandeln but has never used the title, because of my father's outlawing him and taking over the castle."

Giles, who accepted Julius's version—that Xandeln was part of the Grand Ducal patrimony—looked unconvinced.

Catherine said, "What is the Waldemar crest, Con? I don't believe I know."

"You must have seen it on the arms," Con said. "But you are so used to lions in England that you probably didn't notice. It's a lion too, just one, standing up—what do you call that in English?"

"Rampant," said Giles.

"Rampant!" repeated Con with a laugh. "Yes! Well, I never feel very rampant myself, I must say. Perhaps he's only dancing a jig."

Catherine liked this idea, but Giles was looking scornful again.

The Altenbergs were all out sitting on the lawn. Edward was lying on a rug, reading. He got up when they came across the grass and Giles was pleased that in spite of being slightly the younger, he was the taller of the two. Edward came of a tall family; his uncle, the sandy-haired Duke Gabriel, was lean and tall; his father, the dark Count Gilbert, was massive and tall, but Edward had not quite reached the point of shooting upwards which overtakes boys in their teens. He had a thick thatch of dark hair, straight black brows and fierce gray eyes. But he shook hands with Giles in quite an English manner.

The three children sat on the rug, their elders on chairs. Gabriel's wife Geneviève, or Genny, as he called her, was a pretty, rather untidy young woman, whose wavy brown hair seemed about to escape from its hairpins and fall loose. An energetic redhaired baby was doing his best to assist this process by clutching at it. A small boy of about two was staggering about the lawn chasing a puppy. Like Yolande, Genny came from Valmay, and the conversation was mostly in French.

When he could not read Edward soon got bored sitting still. "Let's go for a row on the lake in the park," he suggested.

Nobody made any objection, except that Con said, "Mind you don't tip my Catherine into the water. I've only one niece so be careful of her!"

So they went into the park and Edward hired one of the little boats. He and Giles took it in turns to row while the other steered. Catherine was merely a passenger, but she did not mind; she liked gazing across the water from near its surface, watching the ducks or the other people in their boats. It seemed hard to believe that only that morning she had sat in court while Rafael was tried for rioting; the riot itself seemed almost like a dream. Then she heard Giles and Edward arguing. They seemed to have got angry with each other very suddenly.

"Well, I think Duke Julius is right," Giles was saying. "The Grand Duke has just let everything slide. Those students weren't important. It's the Republicans who matter and he ought to declare their party illegal. Otherwise there'll be more trouble later."

"The Republicans kept the law," Edward said. "Duke Julius is too fond of keeping order by force. It only makes things worse. Con ought to have exiled him in '48—my father always says so."

"*My* father thinks Duke Julius a more able man than the Grand Duke," said Giles.

"Oh, ability!" said Edward. "It depends what you're able *for*." And he added, with scorn, "Whatever you think of Con, he's straight. Julius isn't."

"Why do you say that?" Giles demanded. "He was brave when his carriage was attacked."

"He's not a coward, I grant you," said Edward. "But he's unscrupulous when he's thwarted. You don't know him. We do."

In their argument they had forgotten the boat and now they nearly had a collision with a citizen and his family, who shouted angrily that they should mind where they were going. So Giles and Edward had to stop quarrelling and look what they were about. By the time they landed the argument, if not forgotten, was not picked up again.

Con was waiting on the shore for them, with the ginger-haired Duke of Nordwick.

"Saw you muffing it, Edward, with that worthy candlestick-maker," said Gabriel d'Altenberg. "What's the damage?"

"I don't think even the paint's scratched," said Edward, examining the boat.

"Stop it out of your pocket money if it is, " said Gabriel, with a wink at Catherine. He handed some silver to the man in charge of the boats and they walked up to Con's trap, which a groom had brought into the park.

"Edward's very political," Catherine told Giles as they drove home. "His father is Foreign Minister. That's right, isn't it, Con?"

"Yes, and I only wish he could be Minister of the Interior as well," said Con. "The one they put in after

I sacked Baron d'Hautrec is hopeless. He's mismanaged this grain registration and put half the peasants against the government. It only needed a bit of explaining; it's a measure against famine. There was no trouble at Nordwick, where Gabriel did some talking himself for once, the lazy hound. No trouble at Xandeln, where they're even more old-fashioned. Perhaps because Rafael *wasn't* there to do any talking!" He laughed. He seemed in good spirits and less worried than he had been since their arrival in Letzenstein.

The Hawthornes were invited both to the re-opening of St. Michael's church and to the christening, for which they were to return to the palace chapel, so that Yolande could be present without going out in a carriage. Catherine was rather preoccupied by her duties as godmother and nervous of all the Grand Ducal relations who would be watching. But once at St. Michael's she forgot her apprehensions in her love for the ritual and ceremony of the ancient order of chivalry.

As they walked up the big barnlike church with its high vaulted roof, she saw Jeanne and Paul, in their best clothes, sitting near the back. Jeanne's face had a slightly strained expression and Catherine guessed that she felt strange in this aristocratic and rich company.

The mass was to be sung by the chaplain of the order, but the new Archbishop was present; he sat on a throne at the side of the sanctuary, a solid energetic man in his fifties, more like an administrator than the old Archbishop, who had been a nobleman, at home in courts and palaces, delegating most of his ecclesiastical duties to other priests.

It seemed strange to see Rafael with the knights of

the order, even though she had been present on the occasion when Constant, newly Grand Duke, had made him one. It was not that he looked out of place; on the contrary, dressed in the high-necked white tunic and long crimson mantle with its crusader's cross on the shoulder, the great star sparkling on its chain round his neck, he looked for once the son of a Grand Duke of Letzenstein, as in fact he was.

Catherine suddenly realized why Julius's political differences with him were spiced with personal resentment. Not that anybody could think Rafael handsome, like Julius. Long and thin, with his narrow bony face and close set keen blue eyes, he would always look odd, wherever he was, whatever his manner of dress. But somehow belted tunic and breeches and buckled shoes seemed natural wear to him and the long mantle disguised his awkward gait, though he had not brought his stick into the church. Gazing at him, Catherine understood why people in Letzenstein never thought of him as an artist but as someone who could have been, still perhaps could be, Grand Duke, as his father had been.

Kneeling in his place, his face looked serious, even austere, but when he sat back in his stall he began to stare round the church, looking for Jeanne, Catherine guessed; when he caught sight of her, she almost thought he was going to wave, but he only smiled.

Aunt Eleanor remarked, "How strange to allow that man to take part in an occasion like this, after that disgraceful episode in the square."

And Giles said scornfully, "However did he get into this order?"

"He saved Con's life!" Catherine said, finding it

difficult to keep her indignation to a whisper. "And stopped a riot when Julius declared me Grand Duchess."

"Oh, he can *stop* them too, can he?" said Giles.

No incident disturbed the high mass for Saint Louis, King of France, a ceremony at which the crusader king would have felt quite at home. They all drove back through the sunny streets, decorated with flags for the Prince's christening, and soon gathered once more in the palace chapel, white and gilded and glittered in rococo style.

Now Catherine felt nervous, because she had to hold the baby. Miss Lacey had looked up the Catholic baptismal rites and Catherine thought she would never remember what to do, what with anointings and lighted candles and white cloths and salt on the tongue—all relics of the rites for adults who were baptized in the early church, Miss Lacey told her.

But in fact nobody expected her to know what to do; things were pushed into her hand, words repeated for her, by priests and servers, while she held Christian Louis Rafael in his long christening robe as carefully as possible. Rafael stood by her and held the candle and anything else that needed to be held; he seemed quite unworried and when the baby yelled at the salt on his tongue, he stopped his crying by snapping his fingers to distract his attention. But still, Catherine was relieved when it was all over and the baby given back to his nurse.

The most alarming event of the day, however, turned out to be the christening luncheon, attended by so many Grand Ducal relations, including Julius Varenshalt and his wife Clara, his sister Imelda and their family connexions. The Archbishop and several other priests were there too. Catherine was glad to find herself seated between Edward and Paul; Giles was on the other side of Edward with another girl in between.

It was a very long table and not everyone was so well situated. Somehow Jeanne had been placed between Julius and the Archbishop's Chaplain, across the table, while Rafael was on their side, further along. The knights had taken off their stars and long mantles, sitting down to luncheon in their high-necked belted tunics.

Jeanne looked isolated, Catherine thought. The chaplain, a little spectacled man with a pointed nose, seemed terrified of her; he must have heard she had been a dancer in theatres. Julius pointedly ignored her. He did not speak to her; what was even more rude, he turned his back on her to talk to the lady the other side of him. Catherine could not enjoy her soup at all for thinking of poor Jeanne, sitting there so silent, insultingly ignored.

While they were still waiting for the next course Rafael suddenly pushed back his chair and got up. Everybody stopped talking and stared. He walked all round the end of the table and up the other side and stopped behind Jeanne's chair. Then he said in French, very loudly and clearly, "Julius, as you appear not to wish to converse with my wife, will you please change places with me?"

"Oh, Raf, never mind," murmured Jeanne, embarrassed.

Julius reddened. He turned in his chair, still not

looking at Jeanne, and said, "If you do not know how to behave in a civilized manner, you should have stayed away."

"It seems to me it is you who do not know how to behave," replied Rafael, his blue eyes glinting. He put his hand on the back of Julius's chair. "Let me recommend you to move at once!"

Julius said angrily, "I'm damned if I move to please you!"

"You know more of your ultimate destination than I do," retorted Rafael. "But for the present, the other side of the table will do."

Julius jumped to his feet. Everyone was watching and listening. It almost looked as if there would be a fight at the christening feast. Indeed, Edward muttered in English, "Go on Raf! Sock him one on the jaw!"

Then Con, apologizing to Yolande's aunt, left his place at the head of the table and came down to them. "Julius! Rafael! Please!" he said, putting a restraining hand on the shoulder of each of his cousins.

It was Rafael who yielded. He leant over towards the Archbishop's chaplain and said, "Well, Monsignor, perhaps you would be so kind as to give me your place, as Cousin Julius will not be parted from his." The chaplain glanced at the Archbishop, who nodded. So he rose, and Rafael took his place. Julius, still red with annoyance, sat down again. Con, on his way back to the head of the table, leaned over Raf's shoulder to say, "I'm sorry, Jeanne."

Rafael could never be angry for long and his annoyance with Julius soon evaporated in high spirits. He turned to his next neighbour, who happened to be

Lady Hawthorne and said cheerfully in English, "So! Lady Autorne! My conversation may not be so edifying as your late neighbor's, but I hope it will amuse you enough to pass the time."

Lady Hawthorne looked at him with distaste but she felt she owed it to the Grand Duke to help smooth over the incident his odd cousin had caused, so she said, with a severely gracious air, "When we visited the Marienwald monastery, Monsieur le Marre, the Abbot showed us a picture of yours."

"Really?" said Raf, with such a good imitation of Sir Walter's English drawl that Catherine was afraid Aunt Eleanor would think he was caricaturing him. She noticed Giles flushing. "Really?" said Raf. "I wonder if he would buy another? I am rather short of cash and they seem to have plenty at Marienwald."

The Archbishop, sitting opposite, was looking at him with disapproval.

"Surely," said Lady Hawthorne, "you would not take money for a religious painting, Monsieur le Marre?"

"Why not?" said Rafael. "If Michelangelo was paid for the Sistine Chapel, who am I to waive the fee? The Church is richer than I am."

Lady Hawthorne felt that her effort to be gracious had gone far enough and she retreated to her other neighbour.

Rafael then amused himself by teasing Julius, interjecting disruptive, though not rude, remarks into his conversation. Julius was still angry and became more angry, refusing to reply at all. Catherine realized that he had no sense of humour. He was affronted and obviously thought Con ought to have turned Rafael and his actress wife out, to please him. Paul and Edward giggled at Raf's comments, which annoyed Julius still more.

Jeanne tried to repress Rafael but he only held her hand under the table so that she dared say no more for fear of further embarrassment.

After lunch was at last over, they left almost at once. Catherine, who had been told to go and rest, went out with them, going through the side door on to the terrace. Jeanne was scolding Rafael all the way, but not crossly. He only laughed, put his arm round her and kissed her between each sentence.

As they went down the steps to the stable yard, Paul carrying Rafael's grand mantle rolled up under his arm, Raf waved his hand to Catherine and cried, "To Xandeln, next week!"

And indeed on the Monday Jeanne, with Silvia Caravelli and Chiara, went off by train to Xandeln. Because of the little girl's recent operation Con lent a carriage to take them to the station and he took Catherine with him to see them off. Somehow Rafael and Paul squeezed in too, wearing their painting gear. Raf was staying behind to try to finish the Dragon on the back wall of the church. Toby, of course, insisted on coming too; Raf held him on his knee.

"We'll give you a lift to Xandeln to-morrow, Raf," said Con, "if you can get your painting done in time."

"Give me a lift to the wharf now and I might," said Rafael.

So after the train had gone the carriage drove from the station round to the river wharf and stopped near the converted warehouse.

"Shall we have a look, Catherine?" said Con, and he jumped out. "I haven't seen your cartoon for years, Raf. Have you put me on the road to hell yet? Now that I'm an established figure?"

Raf laughed. "I mean to alter the faces a bit," he said. "So that no one can recognize my youthful rash judgments."

They went through the door and stopped short.

The two ladders from the scaffolding were propped against the wall on the left and two workmen were standing on them, wielding wide brushes of whitewash. There was already a large uneven patch of white, beginning to dry at the corner, all over the frieze of figures.

Rafael stared in silence for a moment and then he went and spoke to the painters in dialect. One of them turned his head and replied, waving his brush.

"He says the Abbé ordered it," said Con to Catherine. "Seems strange to me—Abbé Félix has always admired Raf's work. In fact he paid for the paint and used often to give Raf his meals too, for of course he wouldn't take any money for his work here."

Rafael came back to them. "Paul, just run across and see if Félix is in," he said. Then he sat down on the end of a bench and watched the painters blotting out his figures, in silence.

In a few moments Paul returned with the Abbé, a man about ten years older than Rafael, with thinning hair and rimless glasses. He looked unhappy.

"Rafael! Disaster!" he said. "It's the new Archbishop. Yesterday he suddenly came here for the first time. He ordered me to remove your paintings. I wanted to talk to you first but he said I must start at once. In fact he sent one of his priests down this morning to see if I had. What could I do? He is the Archbishop."

"All?" said Rafael, looking round the walls.

"All!" said Abbé Félix sadly. "I said, 'But not the Christ!' But no, he did not like this figure above the altar to be the humiliated Christ. 'If this is a judgment, where is the judge?' That's what he said. 'This is a defeated man,' he said."

Rafael stared at the figure he had painted. "Yes, a defeated man," he repeated slowly.

"Look here," said Con. "We must talk about this with the Archbishop."

The Abbé suddenly realizing who he was, bowed and said, "It is good of you, sir, to offer to intervene. But the Archbishop was angry. He called it a political painting, done by an infidel. I said, No indeed, how often you were here at my mass, Rafael, yes when there was no one else, sometimes. But it went for nothing. He was determined it should all go."

"He has the right," said Rafael. "Well!" He got up. "No more work for us, Paul. We could have gone to Xandeln today."

Paul looked as if he were going to cry. He turned to Con. "Can't you stop it, sir?" he pleaded.

"I can't cancel the Archbishop's orders," said Con. "But I will see him."

"Don't quarrel with the Archbishop on my account," said Rafael. He went to the corner where he had left his brushes, packed them into the old satchel that lay there and slung it over his shoulder. Then he went outside without looking back and they heard him calling for Toby.

The others followed and the Abbé began once more to lament the destruction. "This figure of Christ has often been an inspiration to me," he said. "I think of that text that comes in the Sacred Heart mass: 'They shall look on him whom they have pierced.'"

"What does it matter about the painting, Félix?" said Rafael. "There's only one image of God that must not be defaced—man, any man. But I'm sorry you'll have bare walls again for St. Michael's feast."

He took Toby's hand and started off up the hill.

Con called out, "Let me drive you, Raf."

But Raf shook his head. "I'd rather walk. I'll see you tomorrow."

He went on, and Paul ran after him, not saying anything.

Catherine felt sad as they climbed into the carriage again. "To think he's been doing it all these years and now it can be spoilt in just a few hours," she said. "And by the Archbishop too."

"Of course I will do my best with him," Con said. "But he's always on the watch for interference by civil rulers with what he calls the Church's rights. And of course Raf did put caricatures of certain magnates on the wall, when he was younger and angrier and was living here among the dockers and derelicts. If there had been a Republican party then, I think he would have belonged to it. I sometimes wonder if my accession hasn't cramped Raf's style!"

But Catherine could only think of that blank whitewash, covering up the images of the lost and the blessed, the dragon and the angel, and the man who was defeated by men.

7

Fair at Xandeln

THE NEXT DAY they all went down to Xandeln, Catherine travelling with the Hawthornes. Rafael had, after all, gone the day before, taking Paul and Toby by the afternoon train. He sent a message to Con by Alphonse, scribbling that Toby was disappointed not to go by train and there was now no reason for him to stay longer in Felsenbourg.

Catherine was irritated because the Hawthornes insisted on regarding Xandeln as "the summer palace of the Grand Dukes" and therefore as belonging to Con; this view they had picked up from Duke Julius, who had given them the impression that Rafael and Jeanne were allowed to live there merely as official caretakers for Constant, well-known for his generosity to his scapegrace cousin. However often Catherine said that the castle was Rafael's, they did not believe her.

Of course when Xandeln came in sight they were surprised to find that it was not a summer palace but only a large house of the late seventeenth century, built into the ruins of an ancient castle. Duke Julius's palladian mansion would have held two or three houses the size of Xandeln.

Catherine had only seen it in winter, covered in snow. Now, as they rounded a bend in the valley and saw the great loop in the river, the long bridge with the village crowded round the spired church at its end, and up on its mound the old yellow stone house growing out of and into the crumbling grey ruins, she caught her breath at the beauty of the place—far more beautiful now among leaves and flowers and apple trees even than she remembered it.

The Grand Ducal carriage with its four fine black horses was ahead of them, but it was not travelling fast and they crossed the bridge not far behind and drove up the winding white road and in at the gates. There was hardly room for a drive; they were immediately in a wide graveled sweep in front of the steps before the house.

On this flight of wide steps stood a motley throng of people, everyone who was living in the castle, in fact, with a lot of children of assorted sizes in front who were waving bunches of yellow broom and cheering. Rafael and Jeanne were standing in the middle at the bottom of the steps, ready to welcome Con and Yolande. Jeanne was wearing the sort of dress the country women wore at festivals, with a full skirt, an embroidered bodice and a white blouse with big sleeves. It suited her strong active figure very well, Catherine thought. Raf was wearing light trousers and a waistcoat embroidered like Jeanne's bodice, with no coat over his white shirt. For once he looked quite clean and tidy. But neither of them looked like landowners.

All the children clapped when Con and Yolande came up the steps. They clapped again for Catherine and the Hawthornes and then all crowded into the hall after them.

The hall had been part of the original castle and was big and high, with a hammer beam roof, long tables, and old weapons hanging on the walls. A wooden staircase with carved posts leading up to a gallery had been put in when the house was rebuilt.

There was a babel of chatter from the servants as well as the children. Con knew them all well and was soon talking to them, asking after their families and being shown a new baby which had arrived since his last visit. So then he took his own baby from the nurse and showed him round with great pride.

The talk was all in the Letzensteiner German, more familiar to the country people than French. Presently the English family were taken upstairs by a smiling maid, remembered by Catherine as the one who had told her, in halting French, that Rafael had been rescued from Julius's guards by the villagers: how pleased she had been at that news!

Catherine had the same room, with the canopied bed and the le Marre crest of the phoenix embroidered on the canopy.

She went out into the passage and nearly ran into Paul, sent to fetch her and Giles down to luncheon. Both the long tables in the hall were set.

"The Mayor's coming, there he is," said Paul, pointing out a fat smiling redfaced man. "And the Curé, of course. It's a celebration for the new prince's birth. Everybody at Xandeln feels Con belongs to them, since he's been coming here ever since he was a boy, when Grand Duke Marius was alive."

"Should you call the Grand Duke by his short name?" Giles irritatingly demanded. He had told Catherine that Paul was "nobody"—just the son of a Letzenstein artist and a middle class woman from London.

Paul flushed. "He told me to," he said.

"He likes to be called Con by his friends," said Catherine. "He didn't want me even to call him uncle, so I don't."

The celebration lunch was a good one and went on a long time; in fact, most people stayed talking over their wine after Con and Yolande had left the table. The visitors went into a sitting room for coffee, where they could be more at ease. It had windows opening into the garden at the side of the house and some armchairs and a couch. As Catherine knew, in the rest of the castle nearly all the furniture was wooden and hard.

Xandeln was a very wooden house altogether, with wooden panelling and shutters, floors without carpets, and hardly anything was painted. The panelling, of light kinds of wood, did not darken the walls. With its rows of tall casement windows the house was full of light.

Later the children went outside and Paul showed them the garden and the stables and then took them down through shelved vegetable plots to a swiftly flowing river. This was not the big river navigable to barges, but one which came rushing down from the hills to join it, making Xandeln almost an island. A footbridge crossed it, and Catherine realized that this was the one she had crossed at night in January last year, coming down from the moor in a snowstorm with Rafael and

Edward d'Altenberg and Albert from Xandeln station. Now the sun shone and the banks were green.

They walked along a narrow path till they reached the place where the little river ran into the big one, just at the bend of the loop where the streams flowed together to join further along the Moselle and then the Rhine. It made a wide expanse of water, and as the high crags on the right towered above there was a ferry. Thus the people from villages to the north could cross to Xandeln without either climbing over the moor to get over the little river or going round by the main road following the bends of the big river to the long bridge.

They sat down on a bench to rest and Paul pointed across at the ferryman's cottage. "That's where we stayed when we escaped from the frontier guards in February '48," he said. "My English uncle had Raf arrested at the frontier but we got out of the station window and walked here in the dark. The river was too high to cross so we stayed the night with Claus the ferryman. We all had to sleep in one room—it was funny!"

"What, Jeanne too?" Catherine asked.

"Yes, Jeanne and Christie Wilkin slept in one bed and Raf and I slept in the other," said Paul. "Jeanne had a kitten from Paris, too. Christie's coming to stay soon. She often does because she's at school in Letzenstein now. Her father is the director of an engineering firm and they keep building railways in this part of the world. Raf calls him the Railway King."

"Your guardian seems to spend a lot of his time being arrested," remarked Giles.

"Yes, doesn't he?" said Paul, evidently not taking this as an insult. "But he's very good at escaping. The other day he said he thought Venice was the only place he'd lived in where he hadn't been arrested, and even from there, you see, he had to escape."

As they climbed up the winding track from the ferry to the castle Catherine asked Paul about last summer, when Jeanne and Rafael, just after they had married, had gone back to Paris to fetch a fatherless family called Brac from the slums there, and had got caught up in the second French revolution of 1848, in June and July.

"It was much worse than the February one," Paul said. "At the end people were simply massacred. I didn't see any of that, thank God. Raf made us stay indoors and he only went out to get food for us. We had to fetch every drop of water in a bucket, and they were selling that too. And the Brac baby kept crying. And then, when it was safe to leave, we had practically no money left, so Raf got a cart and we came home, all the way, in that old cart, with one horse! Luckily it was summer. And luckily too that Raf was brought up in the country, so he knows all about horses. I was scared stiff of them at first!"

This confession increased Giles's sense of superiority to Paul; he could not imagine any boy being afraid of horses.

They walked round from the back of the castle to the garden at the side and found Sir Walter and Lady Hawthorne sitting on one wooden seat and Con and Yolande on another. Jeanne was not there but Rafael was lying on the grass, lazily fighting off Toby and a puppy, who were scrambling all over him.

Catherine sat down beside him and said, "Paul's been

telling us your adventures in the Paris revolutions last year."

Paul said, "You haven't really told us about Venice yet."

"Another time," said Raf.

"In Venezia," said Toby, sitting up, "There wasn't enough dinner, *ever*. And everybody was sick. I was sick. Poor Luca, he was very sick."

"Luca had cholera," said Rafael. "Toby was just sick. It's an activity he's all too good at."

"I was sick in the train yesterday," announced Toby. "And then I was sick in bed. So I got into Raf's bed."

"And then he was sick in our bed," said Raf. "End of conversation about being sick, Toby, please."

Aunt Eleanor now decided to go indoors and Sir Walter went with her. Everybody immediately looked more comfortable and Catherine realized that her English relations were having a dampening effect on the party and anxiously wondered if it would spoil Con's holiday. Jeanne came back and the talk became French.

Presently Paul offered to show the children the ruins of the old castle and Toby went with them, even all the way up the one tower that was not ruined. From there they had a wide view of the fertile valley and across to the moorland, where on the ridge a single standing stone stuck up like an old tooth.

"*Rocher Maudit*," murmured Catherine, remembering how she and Edward had stumbled up to it in the snowstorm at night. Now the moorland was blooming with heather and gorse and broom. Again the strangeness of time passing sent a shiver down her back and she followed the others down the spiral stair of the tower in silence. The stone steps were worn down in waves by the passing of feet, but the feet were long gone, the people were gone.

Outside in the ruins they came upon Luca and Silvia sitting on a crumbling wall, watching Chiara pick daisies. Gaetano was perched on a higher piece of masonry, plucking a guitar. Catherine had not seen him since the riot.

She went up and asked how they were, hearing that Chiara seemed to be regaining her sight, though they had to be careful of her.

"And what did you do about Gaetano's handcuffs?" she asked.

"Oh, he had to wait for the smith here to get at them!" said Luca. "It was awkward for him, but I think he deserved something for leading Rafael into such trouble, don't you? I was angry with him. But! He takes no notice of an old fellow like me."

"How did you get here?" Catherine wanted to know. "Surely people noticed his handcuffs?"

"Didn't Raf tell you? He put us on a boat—one of those big barges. We stayed below in the cabin till we got off here at Xandeln. Raf, he seems to know everyone. He knew this barge captain. 'It was my good luck he was passing,' he said. And it is true—Raffaelle, he has good luck."

"It's not surprising he knew the boatman," said Paul. "Because whenever he was in Felsenbourg for years past he lived down there on the wharf, usually at the Ship Inn. It wasn't safe for him in the upper town, you see, while Grand Duke Edmond was alive." Talking of the wharf reminded him of the disaster to the painting and gloomily he told Luca about it. "And I've asked Con and he says the Archbishop won't change his mind. He even said to Con, 'Why do you allow such a man in your house, an infidel who puts a disbelieving doctor among the blessed and a pious mine-owner on the road to hell!' "

Luca smiled. "He seems a stupid man, your Archbishop," he said. "In Venezia I noticed that Raf went to the mass. It's not common practice among our liberals, though we have our great writer Alessandro Manzoni, author of the historical novel *I Promessi Sposi*—the Betrothed. He is both liberal and Catholic. But Rafael has become much more believing since his fall in the mountains, when he would have died if those monks had not saved him. He makes a joke of it, saying it was the only way he could reward them—his penitence! But I know he is truly converted. It shows in many ways."

A bell began tolling somewhere in the golden summer evening; three tolls and a pause, three more, and again.

"Angelus," said Paul. "I must go back. I have jobs to do now, helping with the children—the orphans."

"What, you have to be a nursemaid?" Giles said.

"I like to help Jeanne," Paul said, flushing slightly.

Catherine soon found it was Jeanne who kept the family of orphans and cripples going, helped by Thérèse Brac, the mother of the French family, and by some other, local women. There were only about twenty children and half a dozen elderly people, but someone else was always being added to the family. Toby was the latest, at first a little puzzled to find Raf had so many other children at Xandeln. He stuck all the closer to him and followed him everywhere like a little dog.

But when Catherine said to Jeanne, "You do everything for the orphans," she would not have it.

"They missed Raf when he was not here," she said. "They talk to him. He plays with them, tells them stories."

After being away the whole summer Rafael had a lot to do at Xandeln, but he never seemed in a hurry and found time somehow to do things with the visiting children, to show the boys where to fish or the safest places to bathe in the little river, which, although it ran so fast, was a more favoured haunt than the big one, sailed on by barges. In the mornings he often went out in a trap to some farm and Con went with him. Everything he did and the way he did it confirmed the Hawthornes' impression that he was running the castle for Con, as a kind of steward.

Christie Wilkin arrived the day after Catherine. She was about a year younger, a small sturdy neat girl with yellow curls and a tilted nose and shrewd grey eyes. Her father, whom Raf called the Railway King, brought her by train, but he only stayed one night. He was a big fat man, energetic and jolly, and not at all a gentleman. Christie, who had been at school near Paris before coming to the one in Letzenstein, was better at speaking French than Catherine, which was lucky for her, as she was quite a chatterbox.

Catherine, as usual, was shy of meeting a new person, but Christie was not at all shy. When she first came in at the door she rushed at Jeanne and kissed her and then rushed at Raf and kissed him and finally kissed Paul, rather to his embarrassment. She was to sleep in Catherine's room and while they were unpacking her things she talked away happily.

"Isn't it marvellous that Raf got away from Venice?" she said. "But he always does get away, doesn't he? My Papa says he must have been born lucky—a cat with nine lives."

Catherine was rather jealous to find that Christie had been a bridesmaid at the wedding of Rafael and Jeanne in the May of 1848. "What was it like?" she asked, watching Christie pull things out of her canvas covered trunk and fling them on her bed in a careless way.

"Oh, everybody sang and danced for hours and ate and ate—the whole village," said Christie. "Con and Yolande danced with all sorts of people, and Jeanne danced with Albert from the station! But Raf couldn't dance, of course, so she didn't so much—they walked about talking to people. He's much better this year, isn't he? Doesn't have to use his stick all the time now—only when he's tired."

The next moment she caught sight of Miche, the Parisian kitten, out of the window; he was now a slinky, sleek black cat and had left his slum origins behind him. "Miche!" cried Christie ecstatically and rushed downstairs to capture and embrace him.

Catherine presently found she rather enjoyed Christie's bouncing confidence, though she never ceased to be amazed at her frankness. But Christie did not hit it off with Giles. "He's stuck up," she said. And of her Giles said, "She's so saucy."

Xandeln echoed with the quarrels and laughter of

children. And yet it was somehow a peaceful place. There were moments, there were corners, where there was silence and sunlight, and Catherine occasionally retreated to brood alone, gazing dreamily over the wide country, where the harvests were all coming home.

Only two days after their arrival Sir Walter had a letter from the ambassador in Brussels, who wanted to consult him urgently in connexion with the mission he had been engaged on earlier that summer. Since the time for their return to England was well ahead, Catherine begged to be allowed to stay on at Xandeln, and when Con and Yolande joined in her plea, the Hawthornes were ready to agree. They still thought the castle belonged to Constant, as Grand Duke; he certainly had first place there, sitting at the head of the table. Rafael and Jeanne le Marre, though undesirable acquaintances, were less disreputable, they thought, and certainly much more busy in this country place. Miss Lacey would keep an eye on Catherine's behaviour. Yes, she could stay.

Catherine was delighted, though she was less pleased to discover that Giles was to stay too. Giles himself was in two minds. He still felt superior to all these foreigners but he did not want to go back to Brussels just when they were staying in the country where he could ride and fish and swim. On the whole, he wanted to stay.

So Sir Walter and Lady Hawthorne left on Thursday afternoon, taking Adèle and Wilcox with them, and Catherine felt a universal sigh of relief went up at their departure, though nothing changed except that

Con went about in shirtsleeves like Raf and Yolande put on a blouse like Jeanne's, and everybody laughed even more than before.

Saturday was the first of September. When Giles came in to breakfast he was greeted with a chorus.

"Happy feast!" They all shouted it in English. "Happy feast, Giles!"

He was quite bewildered. "What do you mean? It's not my birthday."

"It's your name-day, your saint's day," said Rafael. "St. Giles, his day."

"Oh," said Giles. "Thank you."

"And we can celebrate it well, Giles," said Con. "Here is one thing that unites two very different places—Oxford and Xandeln! Both have a fair for St. Giles. After breakfast we all go down to the fair."

And go they did, in a variety of traps and carts, down through the village and over the long river bridge and across the railway track to the water meadows beyond, where the fair was held.

The fair was like a yearly sale to the villagers, who were out in force, looking at stuffs and ribbons and braids and things that they did not make themselves. There were toys and cheap jewellery too, and china plates and coffee jugs and pins and scissors and tools. There were also small wooden plaques, carved with figures of Christ revealing his Sacred Heart as a sign of love for all humanity, and of his Blessed Mother and some of the saints.

Catherine was particularly fascinated by a small triptych, where the central panel showed Mary as a tall woman, holding out her mantle protectively above a crowd of little people in medieval dress, all kneeling on the ground by her feet.

"Oh, Raf, what is that?" Catherine said, catching his arm.

"It's the *Mater Misericordiae*—Mother of Mercy, Our Lady of Pity," he said. "It's always been a favourite devotion here. This is copied from an old triptych above an altar in the cathedral." He peered closer. "By a local carver, I think—a good workman too. And you see St. Michael is on the side panel."

"But who is on the other side?" Catherine asked, pointing at the carving of an old man in a rough habit, kneeling on the ground with his arm round a deer's neck—and an arrow was sticking out of his arm.

Rafael smiled. "It is Saint-Gilles!" he said. "Giles, his patron! He was a hermit a long time ago, hundreds of years ago, who lived in a forest near Arles, in Roman France. A Gothic king was out hunting and Saint-Gilles saved a frightened hind by letting the arrow hit him instead. That's the legend anyway! He's always been a popular saint with the people, just as Saint-François was later, who tamed the wolf and preached to the birds—you know him, I'm sure."

"Oh, yes," Catherine said. "But I can't help thinking Giles would have been hunting with the King, shooting the arrow, don't you?"

Rafael laughed. "Do you like this little wooden altar picture, Catherine? So, I will buy it for you, as a souvenir of Xandeln."

"I would love it!" Catherine said with enthusiasm,

and when it was put in a bag and handed to her by the stall-keeper, she hugged it to herself with delight.

But as they walked away together she said, "Raf, what are you going to do about your paintings in Père Félix's church?"

"Can't do anything," he replied. "Well! I suppose in fifty years they'd be washed out anyhow. I shan't last as long as Michelangelo! But I thought I might go in before St. Michael's feast and paint a vine round the walls for Félix, with a few fishes and peacocks, as in the catacombs."

"Why peacocks?" Catherine asked.

"Symbols of immortality," said Raf. "Unlike my paintings!"

Besides the stalls, the main interest of the fair was the horse racing and for this men and boys had come from all over the countryside. The Altenbergs had ridden over from Nordwick, across the uplands on the German side of Letzenstein. It was not far; nothing was far in that small country. But they had made an early start and were having a picnic of sandwiches and beer at the side of the race-course—which was only part of the field marked out by hurdles.

Much to the delight of the country people Con went in for the races along with the farmers and his Altenberg cousins. Gabriel beat him to the post but Con gave him a good race and came in second. Yolande was tremendously pleased, clapping so hard she almost hurt her hands.

"It's so nice for Con to do the things he does so well," she said.

"Gabriel is lighter, otherwise Con might have won,"

said Rafael, who was sitting on the bank with the women and girls, his drawing block on his knee.

Paul was beside him, also drawing. He needed practice with figures and horses. Raf drew lines over Paul's to show him how but Paul did not mind, much to Christie's surprise. "I should hate that!" she said.

"One only learns by making mistakes," Raf said. "Paul's a good learner."

Con and Gabriel came to sit down, teasing each other.

"You see, he thinks it's time to take over as Regent, now he can beat me," said Con.

"What do you mean, Con?" Catherine asked.

"Con rashly asked me to be Regent if anything happens to him," said Gabriel, with a grin. "And just to make things worse for Letzenstein he named my fellow Archangel to share in the guardianship of his children." He gave Rafael a mock cuff on the side of the head. "Have you revoked that, Con, now that Raf has joined the assassins?"

"Of course not!" said Con, with a serious look in his eye as he glanced at Rafael. Catherine guessed he must be thinking of the misunderstanding she had witnessed outside the Angel Inn and remembered how sorry he had been afterwards to have misjudged Rafael's part in the riot.

Raf said, "After all, the only alternative to us is Julius! He can't stand that!"

And all three laughed.

The boys were getting ready to race now. The Altenbergs had lent Giles a pony. It crowned Giles's day that he won the race, ahead of Edward d'Altenberg and all the other local boys.

They went back to the castle in the middle of the day but returned to the fairground in the evening to watch the dancing. Local teams competed, each with their own band of musicians. Catherine was fascinated by the patterns of steps and never-ending tunes. They stayed till dusk turned to dark and the stars came out overhead. And when they went slowly up the hill in the carts and traps, the country people were still dancing and singing down there by the river, ringed round by flaring torches.

Felsenbourg and its troubles seemed far away.

8

Darkness in Summer

FELSENBOURG WAS not far away to its Grand Duke, even on his holiday. Every day a messenger came from the capital, with an escort of mounted Civil Guards; sometimes another came in the evening. Even on Sunday, they came.

Since Rafael had returned to Xandeln he had reopened the chapel in the castle, which was served by two priests too ill to do ordinary parish work but not ill enough to be complete invalids. One was learned and was known as "*le chanoine*" because he had been a Canon of Felsenbourg Cathedral; the other was young, with a bad heart, and Rafael called him Jo-jo—even the children called him Monsieur Jo-jo. He had a clown's face, somehow sad and funny at once; he was the son of a peasant, whose family belonged to Xandeln. It was he who said the later mass this Sunday, to which Catherine went. As she had been baptized a Catholic, she quite often went to mass, even in London. Aunt Eleanor did not mind, so long as the church was a respectable one.

Today Giles went too, out of curiosity, and it was after this mass that he overheard a conversation between

Constant and Rafael as they stood outside the chapel in the sun. They were talking in French, but Giles knew enough to get what he thought was the gist of it.

Con said, "I'm afraid I must go to Felsenbourg tomorrow, Raf, and stay the night. There have been several incidents with explosives, not serious, but the Minister is worried. I'll be back on Tuesday."

"Must you go tomorrow?" said Rafael. "You'll miss the farmers' dinner—their great annual event."

Con smiled. "My only disappointment will be to miss seeing you trying to look knowing about seeds and pests, Raf!"

"Oh, my role is political!" said Rafael. "I told you I wouldn't play the patriarch here. Fraternity is what I am aiming at. We are learning to be republicans at Xandeln!"

"In that case you'll get on better without me!" said Con, with a laugh.

Rafael said, "Can't you come back the same day?"

"Well, Julius is on the programme too," said Con. "He won't go away from Felsenbourg, thinks I ought not to leave it in a crisis, as he insists it is, and I want to have dinner with him and talk things over. He says, what's true, that the new Minister of the Interior is useless."

Rafael pondered this for a moment and then said, "Why don't you sack him? The Minister, I mean. You could make Gilbert d'Altenberg Minister of the Interior and put someone else in as Foreign Minister, now that foreign affairs are calming down. Baron d'Hautrec, for instance. He's got the diplomatic style—he's impressed Sir Walter *Autorne*—and it would be nice to get rid of him, as a neighbor. He's always looking over my shoulder here. He thinks I'm training a cadre of republican farmers—carrying on from where I left off in '48, according to him."

Con laughed. "Fancy a recommendation for Hautrec from you, Raf!" he said. "But it's an idea. He's an able man."

"It's a pity you can't sack Julius," said Rafael. "He's such a fire-eater. But, poor Con! You can't sack your cousins!" He laughed, slapping Con's shoulder, and they walked away, still talking.

Giles could not help thinking that it was true, as Julius had said to him, that Con was influenced by his cousin Rafael le Marre. And what had he been doing in '48, that caused Baron d'Hautrec to suspect him? Later that day Giles was down by the little river, fishing with Paul. It was always easy to get Paul to talk about his guardian, so Giles asked him about the revolutionary crisis in January 1848.

"It was before I knew Raf," said Paul. "Edward d'Altenberg could tell you about it, he went through it all. Did you know Duke Julius arrested Raf here at Xandeln? Well, Edward helped the villagers to rescue him and they went up to a camp in the hills where some farmers were gathered who meant to march to Felsenbourg to demand just prices. There were some foreigners there who wanted to turn it into a proper revolution against the old Grand Duke, who was a reactionary old tyrant. Later, when Raf was recaptured by Varenshalt's men, he was accused of treason—of organizing rebellion. He was nearly sent to the Rotberg fortress and

Julius even threatened him with summary execution—Edward thought he was going to be shot. But because of the revolutionary mob he was only shut up in the cellars of the palace and the servants there, Alphonse and his friends, rescued him."

Paul had got excited, telling the story. "Even when I came to Felsenbourg with him in March," he went on, "Baron d'Hautrec was so anxious to find out about the foreign revolutionaries he had Raf taken out of the Civil gaol, where he was put for kidnapping me, to question him in the Old Fort. But he wouldn't tell them anything."

"Why not? If those men were revolutionaries," demanded Giles.

"Raf thought the Baron and Colonel Stenken, the commandant, much worse men than the rebels," said Paul. "The rebels had good cause against Grand Duke Edmond's government, after all. Most of them were republicans, exiles then, who now belong to the new party, quite all right."

Giles could not feel it was quite all right. When he saw Constant drive off the next morning he hoped Duke Julius would be able to influence him in the opposite direction from Rafael. Since coming to Xandeln he could not help rather liking Con, who was so good at riding and fishing and shooting and all the things that Giles himself enjoyed; besides, he was a very easy-tempered person. But, Giles said to himself, not clever enough, not sufficiently hard-headed to keep control of the forces unloosed in his little country by a year and a half of European revolution and riot.

In the evening Giles hung about in the hall but he

could make nothing of the farmers' dinner since everyone, Rafael included, talked in the Letzensteiner German dialect. It was entirely a men's affair. The farmers were countrymen with weatherbeaten faces but they were not stupid; they looked an independent, determined breed, and Giles could imagine them gathering in the hills to march to Felsenbourg. Today they wore their best clothes for dinner at the castle.

For the first time since he had come to Xandeln Giles saw Rafael take the head of the table where, during the last week, Con had been sitting. And in the farmers' honour Rafael was wearing what Giles thought "proper clothes", such as Gabriel d'Altenberg might wear, except that they were less sporting than Gabriel's style. He even wore a floppy cravat, the first time Giles had seen him in any kind of necktie.

So there he was, greeting the farmers each by name, and behaving like—well, almost like an aristocrat, Giles thought. "My role is political," he had said to Con. And had said too that Baron d'Hautrec had suspected him of organizing a republican cadre. Or a private army— was that nearer the mark? Giles wondered.

Then he had to go and have dinner in the dining room where they usually ate and here he was faced with another surprise. The Italians were present. Although Giles had seen them in the ruins, with Catherine on the first day, he had scarcely seen them since. They did not come to meals or on any expeditions. Yet now here they were, quite at ease, talking and laughing with Jeanne. Yolande was not at dinner; she had retired early upstairs.

Giles asked Paul where they had been all the week.

"Here!" said Paul, laughing. "But of course Raf had to keep them from meeting Con. Luckily Xandeln is full of odd corners where people can hide."

"Do you mean the Grand Duke didn't know they were here?" Giles asked.

"Oh, I daresay he knows," said Paul. "So long as nobody's told him, it doesn't matter. And there's nobody here who would give them away, nobody like Baron d'Hautrec who would hand over Luca Caravelli to the Austrians."

The very next morning laughter died among the Italian fugitives, for the news came of the final capitulation of Venice the week before, and the restoration of Austrian rule there.

"And the Patriarch of Venice ordered a *Te Deum* to be sung in San Marco!" said Luca, with weary bitterness. "Do you wonder if our liberals are out of tune with the Church?"

They were in the garden; Catherine was with them, but not Giles.

"Patriarchs and popes are not the whole Church," said Raf. "Otherwise what would I be doing in it?"

"Your Archbishop, he obviously asks himself that too!" remarked Luca, with a faint smile. Then he went on despondently, "This news makes me feel like a rat, to have left the ship before it sank. Raf, you should have left me there."

"But no!" Rafael said, with conviction. "Daniele Manin himself told you to go. Free, you can do more for Italy than in some Austrian prison. Yes! Bucintoro will sail again! You will write once more for freedom. *Coraggio,* Luca! You know what Mazzini said, at the defeat of Piedmont? 'The war of the kings is over; the war of the people begins.' Italy will be united and free: believe it!"

Luca's sad brown eyes lighted once more. "Ah, Raffaele, you are a better Italian than I am," he said. "Yes, you are right. But—Venezia! Our republic, that terrible siege . . . to fail yet again."

"Defeats must never defeat us," Rafael said.

Catherine wandered away among the ruins, thinking of that distant defeat, the anguish and suffering so hard to believe in while the sun shone from the blue sky. And touching the crumbling stone of the standing tower she wondered what defeats had been endured by the people who lived there long ago. Yet still the tower stood, and their descendants lived on.

Con had sent a messenger that morning to say he hoped to be back in the evening and about the time of the Angelus Catherine, coming round the corner of the house from the garden, saw Rafael and the young priest Monsieur Jo-jo, climbing into a small trap. Paul was holding the horse's head. When Rafael took up the reins, he too climbed in.

"Raf! Where are you going?" Catherine called out.

"Taking Jo-jo to see his mother," said Rafael. "We might meet Con too. It's in the same direction. He always takes the short cut through the gorge to save the bends in the main road where it follows the big river."

He was again wearing his country trousers and blouse with no tie. The trap went off at a leisurely pace along the dusty lane, not down to the village but up behind the ruins into the narrow valley through which the little river rushed down from the hills to join the big one above the ferry.

Dinner time came, but neither Con nor Rafael had returned. The others waited for half an hour and then ate their dinner. Yolande was with them and Giles noticed that the Italians were not. Evidently, expecting the Grand Duke's return, they had retired into hiding again.

After dinner Giles went up to the room he shared with Paul to write to his parents. He told them about winning the race at St. Giles's fair. Because of the moths coming in he shut the window and the shutters when he lit the lamp, so he heard nothing going on outside.

Catherine was wandering about the garden. Now that it was September the evenings were not so long; it was not that they suddenly grew shorter but that the quality of light changed with the slanting of the sun's beams. All round the hills lay solid and beautiful in the golden glow. Then the sun was gone, the sky gleamed greenly at its edges, the dusk turned trees and walls to shadows.

Catherine saw Jeanne, with a shawl round her shoulders, walking about the gravel sweep, and went to join her. She could tell Jeanne was anxious.

"What can have happened, Catherine?" she said. But then she added, "Nothing can have happened to Rafael in his own country."

Suddenly they heard steps on the gravel, hurried steps and heavy. A man was coming in at the gates, walking fast but breathing hard.

Jeanne almost ran towards him.

"Madame!" the countryman began at once, speaking in guttural French. "Madame, the Seigneur sent me to tell you . . . there's been a terrible event."

"But he? Is he well?" Jeanne asked quickly.

"Yes, he is, have no fear for him, madame. It is the Grand Duke . . ."

"Oh no!" Jeanne whispered.

The man stood, trying to get his breath to speak. "Madame, he may not be dead. We do not know. The bridge . . . you know the bridge in the gorge, the narrow one?" He held his hands a few inches apart. "Nobody knows how it was done . . . no one was there. But it blew up! It blew up when the carriage was on it. The carriage went into the river. The groom who was behind, he was killed, madame. He fell on the rocks and we found him dead. But the coachman and the Grand Duke, of them we saw nothing. We have been looking for hours. The Seigneur is still there, looking."

"Oh, what a terrible thing to happen!" Jeanne said. "Poor Yolande—oh, how will I tell her?" After a moment she asked, "How was it that he—that Monsieur le Marre was there?"

"He was going that way, madame, and he was quite near at the time of the explosion. He was first there but he saw nothing of those who did this terrible crime. Lucky it was that there were men who had been working on the road, further up, just going home. They heard the noise and came running and met the Seigneur just by the ridge. I too heard; I was cutting wood on the hill. We have all been searching the river for the

Grand Duke, for he must have been carried away, dead or alive, when he fell. You know how fast it goes there, and it is deep in the gorge too. The bridge is built high because of the floods. So it was a great fall. The horses had to be shot. It is a very deserted place."

Catherine listened in silence and horror. Con, her uncle, blown up, carried away in the river—no, it could not be true. It was too terrible.

"The Seigneur asks you to tell the Grand Duchess, madame, and to say he does not yet despair to find the Grand Duke alive. But I think he will come back now that it grows dark."

Jeanne said, "Yes, I must tell Yolande." And she shivered as they turned back to the house. She caught Catherine's hand as they went. "Oh Catherine! How can men do such evil things?"

She went alone to the room where Yolande was sitting. Catherine hung about in the hall for what seemed a long time, though it was not really long before she heard horses outside and ran to the front door, which still stood open.

There were oil lamps each side of the door and another over the gate; in the dim yellow light of these she saw several countrymen on horses and Rafael among them. She had never seen him riding before and suddenly realized that before his accident on the mountain in Italy he must have been as used to riding everywhere as Con and Gabriel. Now he had difficulty in dismounting. Paul ran to help him. Stiffly and awkwardly he got to the ground and came towards the house, with his hand on Paul's shoulder for support.

As he came slowly up the steps she saw he was soaking wet and muddy, his clothes stuck to him and his face was hollow with tiredness.

Jeanne had come out of the sitting room and she ran to him at once and took his arm to help him to a chair.

He said, "We have found the coachman—his body. We haven't found Con."

Nobody said anything; it was too dreadful an event for words.

Then Yolande came into the hall. She was pale but fully in control of herself. Seeing her coming, Rafael got up from his chair.

"Rafael, did you find anything?" Yolande asked quietly.

"Only this," he said, fumbling in his pocket and holding out Con's big watch, which he wore on a chain in his waistcoat. The glass and face were smashed and the case dented.

Somehow, seeing the broken watch made Catherine want to cry. Her throat hurt, tears burned in her eyes.

But Yolande did not cry. "Who found it? Where was it?" she asked.

"I found it," Rafael said. "It was quite near the bridge, in a shallow place. I think it fell out when he fell. But he could not have fallen there. He would have been killed at once. He must have fallen in the deep part. But we have found nothing more, nor for a good way downstream."

Yolande said, "I don't believe he is dead, Rafael. I don't *feel* it."

Rafael hesitated. "No, nor did I," he said at last. "I had every hope at first of finding him alive."

At first, he had said.

"You can't have gone far enough downstream," said Yolande.

"He could hardly have been carried further and not drowned," Rafael said.

Jeanne made a movement as if to stop him saying any more but Yolande said, "No. I'd rather *know*. Everything you can remember, Rafael, please."

"Well, I set the men to look on shore too, of course," he said, moving so that he could lean on the back of the chair. "I think we found the place where the men hid when they placed the explosive, but we did not find any trace of them. It was quite a difficult engineering job and several must have been involved."

"Please do sit down, Rafael," Yolande said.

"No. I'll wait till I can lie down now," he said. "I've left some men there to watch. I'll go back in the morning. I've told the mayor and he's sent an electric telegraph to Felsenbourg, to the Premier. We can't send one across to Nordwick, unfortunately, but Gabriel will probably hear the news tomorrow. You realize, Yolande, that until we find out what's happened to Con, Gabriel is Regent."

None of them had in fact thought of this.

"I've seen the Captain of the Civil Guard here and he has already started a search for the assassins," said Rafael. "I was afraid that if Con was not killed at once they might have—well, tried to finish the job. But we could find no signs of workmen, from the other direction. If only I had got there just a bit sooner!"

"Then you would have been blown up too," said Paul, who had been standing silently by, all this time.

He too was dirty and pale with tiredness, but not wet. He told Catherine afterwards that Rafael had not allowed him in the river. The current was so strong, he was afraid of Paul's losing his footing and being carried away.

"Now," said Jeanne suddenly. "Everybody go to bed! It is the only thing. We must find strength for tomorrow. Children, upstairs, please! Goodnight, Catherine, dear child."

She kissed Catherine's tear-stained face and sent her upstairs. Christie Wilkin was already in bed and reading by candlelight. She saw Catherine's face and sat up. "Catherine, what's the matter?"

When Catherine told her, she jumped up in her impulsive way and sat beside Catherine on her bed and hugged her. "Oh, what an awful, awful thing to happen! Oh, do you think he is really dead?"

"Yolande doesn't feel that he is," said Catherine, but she felt almost hopeless herself. The groom was killed, the coachman was drowned. The horses had had to be shot. How could Con have escaped?

It was a comfort to have Christie in the same room with her. Although she lay awake for what seemed like hours, seeing again and again in her mind the carriage falling from the blasted bridge and Con's body borne away in the fierce rush of water, she did eventually fall asleep.

And because she had gone to sleep so late, Catherine woke in broad daylight and when she got downstairs she found Rafael had gone back to the gorge at dawn with more men, ropes, nets, poles and rakes.

"He wanted to ride but he just couldn't manage it,"

Paul told her. Paul had been left behind for all his pleading. He was looking pale, with rings round his eyes. "So he went in the trap again."

It was the most dreadful day to live through because nothing happened and at Xandeln they could do nothing to help. The sunshine seemed a mockery. Rafael came back earlier on this day, about Angelus time. He was not so exhausted, because he had left the actual searching to others, and they were still at it, under the direction of the local Civil Guard. But neither the assassins nor their victim had been found.

Rafael had not been back long when the Mayor of Xandeln and several village officials came up the main road, sweating in the still hot summer evening.

"Seigneur! Bad news from Felsenbourg!" said the panting Mayor, wiping his brow with a large handkerchief.

"What now?" Raf said, wearily.

"There has been a *coup d'état*," said the Mayor. "The Duke Julius Varenshalt has been proclaimed Grand Duke."

Rafael jumped to his feet. "What? Julius? The swine!" he cried.

The Mayor waved his hands helplessly. "It seems there was a scene in the Chamber. As you know, it is vacation, but some Deputies were hastily assembled. There was a speech from Baron d'Hautrec and others, I believe, spoke. They asked the Duke to take over the government and save the country. And the Duke agreed."

"How do you know all this?" Rafael asked.

"Seigneur, our own Deputy was in Felsenbourg and

has come back on the train to tell us. We wanted him to come up to you, but his wife would not allow it. Poor man! He is both tired and frightened. He wished to oppose the Duke but did not dare. He says the Duke has declared martial law and will close the frontiers. He intends to declare the Republican Party illegal and exile or imprison anyone connected with it. Now, Monsieur le Marre, what are we to do?"

He looked anxiously at Rafael, evidently expecting immediate directions.

"He has done all this and we don't even know what has happened to poor Con yet!" said Rafael indignantly. "Baron d'Hautrec asked him to take power! Yes! And he asked the Baron to ask him, I've no doubt."

"Like Richard III," murmured Miss Lacey, who was present. "Shakespeare's Richard, I mean."

Rafael smiled, the first time he had since the disaster. "You are just right, Miss Lacey!" he said in English. "Shakespeare always knows!" Then he turned to Jeanne and asked, "Where is Yolande?"

"I am here," Yolande said. She had heard voices and come on out to the landing from her room, where she had been nursing her baby.

Standing up there at the head of the stairs, tall and pale, with her bright hair gleaming, she looked so sad and so beautiful that all of them gazed up at her for a moment in silence. And they stayed silent while she came down to the hall.

Then Rafael went towards her and kissed her hand.

"Yolande, I am afraid you must take the baby and go to Gabriel at Nordwick tomorrow," he said gently. "Julius has usurped the place that belongs to your child, if we no longer have Con with us. Gabriel is the Regent. You must go to him."

Yolande's lips trembled a little. "Must I leave, still not knowing?" she said, almost in a whisper.

"I think you must," said Rafael. "I don't trust Julius. He knows you are here. I think this is what Con would wish. I promise you, as soon as we know anything about what happened to him, we will send you news."

"Yes, I see I ought to do this," said Yolande.

"Madame la Duchesse," said the Mayor. "We are loyal, we in Xandeln. If God has not preserved Constant Waldemar, we accept the Duke of Nordwick as Regent, with you, for the Prince. We will not recognize Varenshalt as Grand Duke."

Yolande thanked him. Then she went back upstairs and Rafael called for wine for the village officials.

Catherine and Paul went out into the garden and saw Giles there with his fishing tackle, checking it over. Giles had been as upset as anyone by the news of Con's disappearance, when he heard of it, and it was partly because he wanted something to do that he now said, "Paul, what about going fishing again?"

"Oh no, I couldn't, not in the little river," Paul said, with a shudder.

Catherine knew he was thinking of Con, carried away in the water, perhaps drowned in it, his body stuck somewhere under the surface. This picture was haunting her mind too. To exorcise it, if only temporarily, she said, "Julius has made himself Grand Duke."

They passed on what they had heard in the hall, Paul filling in the details which Catherine had missed, in all the French talk. "Miss Lacey said it was like Richard the Third in Shakespeare," she said. "Putting up people to ask him to be king."

Giles said, "All the same, Julius would make a better Grand Duke than Gabriel d'Altenberg, don't you think?"

"That's not the point," said Paul. "Con named Gabriel Regent, not Julius. And Julius hasn't even called himself Regent. He's out for himself."

"Why can't you allow Julius to be sincere?" Giles said. "He could think it best for Letzenstein if he takes power."

Paul did not reply; he turned away.

"Paul! Won't you really come fishing in the morning?" Giles said.

"We can't anyway," said Paul, over his shoulder as he went towards the house. "Raf told us not to go beyond the garden."

"Why ever not?" said Giles, irritably.

"He thinks the assassins may still be around," said Paul, turning back. "And he wants to be sure everyone's within reach. You heard him say so, last night . . . oh, no, you weren't there. But you were there this morning."

"What rot!" said Giles. "He is ordering people about now, isn't he? Anyone would think *he* was some kind of a Duke."

"Well, he is the Seigneur here," said Paul. "He has the right to order people about, as you call it, in his own castle."

Giles laughed. He still thought the castle belonged to the Grand Duke. "His own castle!" he said scornfully.

Paul flushed. "Will you stop laughing at Raf?" he said, doubling his fists.

"You think he can never do anything wrong, don't you?" said Giles. "Well, he's not *my* hero and I don't see why I should do as he says. I shall go fishing if I like."

He picked up his tackle, but he went into the house not down to the river.

Paul said, "How can he go on so, at such a time?"

"Giles can be very irritating," Catherine agreed.

They went into the house by way of the sitting room, which had window doors opening on the garden, put in by Rafael's mother; it had been a favourite room of hers and it was she who had brought in the couch and the armchairs. On the wall was a portrait of her sitting in the garden with her husband, the Grand Duke Marius, and Raf, about five years old, in a short jacket with brass buttons, standing between them, looking ready to fight all comers. Jeanne was fond of this picture and called it "funny little Raf." Toby was puzzled by it, often going to have a look. "But he's smaller than me," he said. His fascination was increased when Raf found the little jacket, which Toby could just get into if he left it open. "Nothing's ever thrown away here," Rafael had said.

Toby was in the hall now, haunting Raf again; his disappearance each day to the river had revived Toby's fears of loss, his memories of the papa who had gone away on a ship and never come back. As he saw the Mayor off, Raf had Toby by the hand.

As soon as he saw Paul he sent him with a message to the ferryman. The quickest way to Nordwick was by the moor road and the easiest way to reach it was by the ferry. So he planned to send the best carriage the long way round that evening, by Xandeln bridge and northwards, crossing the river again at Tiepol. Then in the morning Yolande could go by the ferry and pick it up the other side. He was too busy to talk to Catherine and later she forgot what Giles had said about going fishing.

∽ 9 ∾

Two Escapes

GILES WOKE UP early on that Thursday morning, September 6th. Outside there was a thin mist, but with a feeling of the sun coming through and a fine day to come. Paul was not in his bed; he had slipped out already.

"I *will* go fishing," Giles thought. "No one would come so near the castle."

He got up, pulled on his oldest clothes, took his rod and tackle and went out on the landing. He could hear sounds at the back of the house but no one was in the great hall. So he went quickly and quietly down the staircase and out of the open front door, down the dewy steps and round the corner to the rose garden— no roses there now.

Softness, quietness, misty morning light.

Giles went through the archway into the old ruins. The grass was long here, and wet, as he picked his way to the gap where a path led down the steep hill to the little river, near the wooden footbridge. This was where he had fished before, with Paul.

He had only gone a few yards down the path when he heard someone call him. "Giles!"

He turned round. Rafael le Marre was standing in the gap, with his stick in his hand. The exertions of the last few days had reduced him to using it again.

"Giles, come here, please."

Giles thought of just going on, but perhaps Rafael would send someone after him and it would be ignominious to be brought back. So he turned and climbed up the path again, without saying a word, and looking sulky.

"Surely you heard me say yesterday that no one was to go beyond the garden?" said Rafael. He did not sound angry but he was quite serious.

"Oh, I didn't realize you meant us too when you said *'mes enfants'* " said Giles, rather insolently.

"Didn't you?" said Rafael and Giles felt himself flushing.

"I don't see why you should tell me what to do," he said crossly.

"I am responsible for you, Giles, since your father is not here," said Rafael. "I think you did know my wish, because Paul repeated it to you."

"Sneak," muttered Giles, realizing that Paul must have told Rafael what he had said about going fishing.

"What is that you say? Snake?" Rafael said, puzzled by the slang word.

"No—sneak," said Giles. "Paul must have given me away to you."

Rafael said, "Come Giles, be not angry with Paul. He knows this rule is not made for nothing. Come with me, please."

He started off, back through the ruins and the garden and into the house. Giles followed him, wondering what he was going to do; still more so when they climbed the stairs and went towards his room. He eyed Rafael's long stick, which he had seen him wield like a weapon in the riot and rather hoped he was not going to be beaten with it.

However, Rafael only leant on it when they reached Giles's room and looked at him with his very blue piercing eyes. Somehow Giles felt uncomfortable.

"Giles, I am too busy to watch you," Rafael said. "I am sorry I cannot trust you to obey my wish. So you must stay in your room for today. I will tell Max to bring your meals up here."

He took the key out of the lock on the inside of the door and put it in again on the outside.

"You're going to lock me in?" said Giles, incredulously.

"Just so, I am," said Rafael. He glanced round. "Yes, you have books. I will release you this evening when I am at home."

He went out and Giles heard him lock the door.

So there he was, locked up for the day. He was brought his breakfast soon after, but he was too cross to talk to the man who brought it, a sturdy manservant with greying hair, whom Giles had often seen about.

The morning seemed the longest he had ever spent. For much of it he sat in the open window looking out. He watched while Yolande, the baby and his nurse, and some of Constant's personal servants came out to go down to the river. Some of the Xandeln women standing round were crying.

Soon after the Grand Duchess left, Giles saw Rafael

go out in the trap, with Paul as usual beside him, going the way to the gorge. An hour or two later, as he glanced up from his book, he saw they had returned and had stopped by the gates where two strange looking figures in ragged blackened clothes, with rough leggings, were standing. Giles watched. Rafael got down from the trap to talk to these men; he seemed excited, catching one by the arm and questioning him. Paul seemed unmoved; he stood by, holding the horse, and Giles guessed that the talk was in dialect. Paul was bilingual in French and English but he knew no German.

At last Rafael sent the men away—with money, Giles thought. He shouted out, "*Holà!* Antoine!" till a groom appeared to take over the horse and trap for him. Then he and Paul walked towards the house.

Giles moved back so as not to be seen at the window; he did not want any conversation with Rafael or Paul at the moment. He had no intention of listening to their talk but he found himself overhearing it. They were talking in English. This was odd, for Rafael talked French with Paul, unless he did not want everyone to know what he was saying.

Now Giles heard Paul say, "But Raf, if he is not dead, why didn't you go at once and fetch him back here?"

Not dead! Surely it must be the Grand Duke they were talking about? Giles was glad to hear that Constant, whom he could not help liking, might be alive after all. But then he heard Rafael's voice, speaking rather quietly.

"Listen, Paul, this game has become very dangerous,"

he was saying. "While he was thought to be dead the situation has changed. Now, if he comes to life, who knows what will happen? No, it must not be known that he lives. We do not yet know how badly he is injured. I will bring him down under cover of darkness. Here we can hide him, for days if need be. No one need know . . ."

Giles heard no more. Cautiously looking out he saw that they had gone round the corner of the house into the rose garden.

Giles's heart beat fast. What had he overheard? It seemed to him strange, even sinister. Rafael had just learned from those queer looking men that Con was alive; yet he was proposing to wait till night to bring him back to the castle and then he was going to hide him, so that no one should know he was alive. Why should he do this? Why, thought Giles, unless he himself had some plot or scheme about the Grand Duchy which would be spoiled if his cousin was known to be alive.

Giles had not been in the hall the night Rafael came back from the first search for Con, or when the Mayor had brought the news of Julius's *coup* in the capital. He had always thought it strange that Raf had been first on the spot after the explosion. He had heard much from Julius about Rafael's rebel activities and his cunning in hiding his tracks, so that Baron d'Hautrec had never succeeded in getting evidence against him under Grand Duke Edmond. Julius made no secret of the fact that he thought his cousin Constant a bit of a fool, but he had no such illusions about his cousin Rafael. He had told Giles that Rafael was a "playactor"—he took people in with his casual joking manner, but really he was a calculating person, always keeping his own end in view.

All this came back to Giles now as he sat by the window pondering what he had overheard. He was quite startled when Max came in with his lunch on a tray. It was cold meat and fruit and Max seemed willing to stay and talk while he ate. Giles decided to pump him. Max spoke French, so Giles asked him in French whether Rafael had not come back from the gorge already.

"Yes—there is nothing he can do there now," said Max, sadly. "But I am afraid, Monsieur Giles, the Seigneur says that all the same you are to stay here till evening as he ordered. He will take the key from me now and let you out himself."

"Nothing has been found?" Giles said.

"No," said Max, heavily. "And now, only the Grand Duke's body can be found. He cannot be living."

Giles thought otherwise, but he said nothing. He tried another line. "Why do you call Rafael le Marre Seigneur?" he asked.

"Because he is," said Max, surprised. "He is, and always has been—since his noble father's death—the Seigneur of Xandeln."

"But after his father's death it belonged to the Grand Duke, surely?" said Giles.

"Oh, it is true that the Waldemar took the castle," said Max scornfully. "Without right! It did not make Monsieur Rafael any the less the Seigneur, for us, the le Marre people. Prince Constant knew this. He did a lot for us here but he knew we all thought so—indeed, he recognized Monsieur Rafael's right himself."

"But his mother was only a commoner," Giles said.

"*Tant pis!*" said Max, smiling. "You must know, Monsieur Giles, that many of us think that Monsieur Rafael should be not only Seigneur of Xandeln but Grand Duke in Letzenstein. But he was only a child when his father died and Edmond Waldemar did what Julius Varenshalt has now done—made himself Grand Duke, although there was a child to inherit."

Giles asked, "Does Monsieur le Marre think that too?"

Max shrugged. "No, he has always been for Constant Waldemar; they were friends from childhood," he said. "But now that Constant is dead, some of us would prefer Monsieur Rafael to Duke Julius, I can tell you. Even to a Regency of Duke Gabriel d'Altenberg, for though he is someone we all like, he is not the kind to be a ruler."

"And you think Monsieur le Marre is?" said Giles, surprised.

"Why not?" said Max. "He knows our country and our history and he knows the world of our day. Some people think he is eccentric but that is mostly his high spirits. To me, there is a certain air of the prince in the way he laughs at conventions. And he is no fool, our Seigneur. He is a shrewd man, a practical man, for all his love of his art. Everyone knew he was opposed to Grand Duke Edmond's government but they could never catch him out, those city fellows, and the police."

When Max went away Giles was left feeling even more suspicious of Rafael's intentions with regard to Constant. Suppose he was planning a revolution, with himself as leader, who would then take over when the others were out of the way? If Con were badly injured and hidden at Xandeln, who would know if he died, since everyone thought him dead already?

Looking out of the window Giles noticed how thick and strong were the stems of the old magnolia tree trained up the wall by his room. "I believe I could climb down there," he thought.

Almost at once the plan formed in his mind. He would climb out, go down to the station and catch the afternoon train to Felsenbourg. Julius Varenshalt ought to know that Constant Waldemar was alive; well, Giles would tell him.

Giles collected all his money, and his father had left him a good deal, in case of emergencies. He changed out of his fishing clothes into a more respectable suit and put on a cap. If he was caught before he left the grounds he would just pretend he was sick of being shut up in his room. Rafael le Marre might lock him up again or even cane him with his stick, Giles did not care. He would have made the effort to do something he felt ought to be done.

In fact, he was not caught. Everyone was either clearing up the midday meal or resting after it in the heat of the day. Giles found the first bit the worst—climbing over the sill and trusting himself to the knotty stems of the magnolia. But once he was on the tree and it bore his weight, he climbed down with agility. Then he made himself walk, not run, across the hot gravel sweep and out of the gates, which always stood open in the daytime.

In the village not many people were about and no one had any reason to stop the young English visitor from going to the station. It was a thing English visitors were expected to do; and in fact all the boys at the castle were to be found there at one time or another. Railways were the latest fashionable thing and some boys saved up so as to ride just as far as the next station.

Giles took a ticket to Felsenbourg and sat on a seat on the deserted platform. Presently one or two other people appeared; nobody he knew. The train came in. He got into an empty compartment, warm and stuffy. He opened the window on the other side, looking over the water meadows where the fair had been held last Saturday. The ground was still trodden almost bare of grass where the crowds had been and he could see the circle of the race track where he had won his race, beating Edward d'Altenberg by a neck.

Then the whistle blew, the train gave a jerk, and he was on his way to Felsenbourg.

When Rafael and Paul went round into the garden, they saw Jeanne and Catherine sitting on a bench with their backs to them.

Rafael went quietly up behind them, put an arm around each and said, "What if I were to tell you the most wonderful news in the world?"

"Con!" cried Catherine, turning quite pale. "He wasn't killed!"

"Yes, that's it," Rafael said. He came round and sat on the bench between them, and Paul sat down on the ground. "I've just this moment heard it, from the charcoal burners. They found him, last night."

"But what happened? How was it they found him and not you?" Jeanne said.

"Jeanne, Con is so strong, he got much further than we thought," Rafael said. "Of course you know those poor charcoal burners are not very clever, but at least they know the hills up there and I can tell where they found Con. He can't have been unconscious for long in the river and he must have got out of it below the bend which we put as the furthest mark. And then he must have climbed a long way up the hillside through the woods, probably not really knowing what he was doing. We never looked as high as that."

"But how was it he did not hear you looking for him?"

"That I don't know, but perhaps he had delayed concussion," said Rafael. "From what they say he seemed dazed and ill when they found him—after what? Twenty-four hours lying out on the hillside, I suppose. The poor fellows didn't know who he was—still don't. 'We have found a man, a big man,' they said to me just now. 'A gentleman by his clothes, lying in our woods, terrible bruised he is.' So they came to find me, to know what to do with him."

"They did not bring him down?"

"No, and lucky they didn't," said Rafael. "I was just telling Paul, we must wait till nightfall to do that."

"But why? I don't understand this," said Jeanne.

"Dear Jeanne, you do not know Cousin Julius as I do," said Rafael. "What has he done? He has declared himself not Regent but Grand Duke—or got others so to declare him. He has already proclaimed martial law and proposes to outlaw the Republicans. He has the best part of the army just outside Felsenbourg and the Civil Guard headquarters there. Do you think he is going to give up at once what he has been wanting to gain for so long, power, supreme power in Letzenstein?"

Catherine, following the French as well as she could, said in English, "But Raf, what could he do, if he knew Con was alive?"

"I'm not sure," he answered. "But I do not think he will just shake him by the hand! I think he would try to get rid of him, as he did before."

"Murder him?" said Paul.

"Perhaps not that—yet I am not sure someone like Stenken would not do it for him," said Rafael. "Even if not murder, I think he will try to force Con to leave the country. I could imagine them taking him over the frontier secretly and making away with him there. What I am sure of is that we must get Con over to Nordwick as soon as we can."

"Why do you send everyone to Nordwick?" asked Catherine. "Yolande and the baby, and now Con."

"First because Gabriel has better standing in the country than I," said Rafael. "I am not one of the true aristocracy!" He laughed. "You know, my common blood—just red and not blue!"

Jeanne smiled, understanding his English when she could not follow other people's. She said, in French, "Raf, your blood changes colour to suit the situation!"

"Well, not only is Gabriel blue right through," said Rafael, laughing and reverting to French, "but he has aristocratic English relations. He has also a great many retainers, almost like a private army, especially as they have the best horses in Letzenstein! For Julius, Nordwick is much less vulnerable than Xandeln. Then also the Altenbergs are in with the other ruling families, as

I am not, and Gilbert is a Minister in the government, as at present constituted. Julius meets his match in them. With me, it's not so. I have no position from which to meet Julius, and in fact I am a liability to poor Con and always have been. Not willingly so, but it is from the accident of my birth."

The bell rang for luncheon and they went indoors. As they passed into the sitting room Rafael said, "So please say nothing, any of you, about this discovery. Catherine, you understand?"

Catherine nodded. She alone of the three of them knew what it was like to be a political pawn in Duke Julius's hands. And only she had been in Felsenbourg in January 1848 when Julius had threatened Rafael with summary execution for treason. She was very happy because Con was after all alive but she realized that the time of anxiety was by no means at an end.

Because Max had taken Giles's tray away after lunch nobody knew he had escaped. Rafael sent someone to call off the search in the gorge but he gave no reason for his order. Most people thought he had given up hope of finding the body of the Grand Duke. Some said the murderers must have carried it away.

Although he did not mean to bring Con back till evening Rafael had no intentions of leaving him unaided till then. Giles, in fact, was still in the village when Raf, not knowing that he had escaped, set off with four trusted men and a cart. Jeanne went with them, carrying a basket of things she thought might be needed. Paul was allowed to go but not the girls, or Toby, much to his dismay. "Why can't I go on the picnic?" he kept asking.

It was Luca Caravelli who finally carried him off to play with Chiara in the garden; he fetched a can of water and started them off making mud pies and pots. Catherine and Christie stayed in the garden too and Christie, when she discovered Luca could speak English, asked him endless questions. It seemed queer to Catherine to talk about Italian hopes and republican defeats when her thoughts were so much occupied with events in Letzenstein, but she found herself listening, all the same, when Luca told about the siege and the three weeks of bombardment which had started in July.

"Raf came in May," he said, "and almost at once we were besieged. Then I got the cholera! What a time! Gaetano was in one of our gun batteries, hardly at home at all. Raf, he nursed me. Then he picked up this little Toby, starving and wild, poor child. There were others too but they were Italian, so he was able to take them to nuns or brothers, to live. Toby had no one and was English, so Raf would bring him, escaping, although that made it more difficult, of course."

From Venice, escape had to be by boat and at night, to slip through the blockade. And even when they reached the mainland there were Austrian troops to evade as they made their way up the mountains to cross into Switzerland.

Toby was listening, while he appeared totally absorbed in the mud bowl he was shaping. Presently he said, "Luca, do you remember those officers, how they went ha-ha, ha-ha, when Raf was pretending to be German?"

Luca laughed. "Yes! That was truly a scene of comedy, Miss Christie. At the time I was too nervous to laugh. We were the nearest thing to being found out. But Raf, he began to talk in German, he was suddenly the German artist—but perfectly! And he amused those Austrian officers so much with his nonsense that they did not notice Gaetano and me, going so quietly away. Then we waited and waited, fearing something was wrong, but it was only the officers would make Raf drink with them and he could not get away."

"And so he was drunk!" cried Toby, waving his mud bowl in the air. "Raf was drunk!"

Miss Lacey, who was present, said, "Dear me, I hope not!"

Luca smiled. "Not very," he said. "He drinks little, so it affects him more easily. But he can act, Raf can! He could be a comedian any day."

It seemed a very long time to Catherine, waiting for evening. It was nowhere near dark at Angelus time, when the bell over the chapel rang its three times three musical tolls, but she walked out to the gates alone in the golden light. She looked back at Giles's window, not seeing him, but not guessing he was not there.

Rafael had not, in the end, waited for dark, for as she stood at the gate Catherine saw the cart coming down the narrow road from the gorge. The men were walking, Jeanne and Rafael riding in the cart. And then she saw someone else, though he was lying down almost out of sight, covered with a woven blanket.

Raf and Jeanne climbed down and Jeanne gave Catherine a hug. "He's going to be all right," she whispered in French. "He must have been concussed and of course he was battered about in the river, but I don't think there's anything else wrong."

Catherine could not see Con now because Raf had pulled the blanket right over his head. The cart was driven to the corner of the house so that no one could have seen when Con was helped out and taken straight into the sitting room through the open doors. When she went in, there he was, lying on the couch.

"Catherine!" said Con, smiling at her. "Catherine, my niece!"

He liked to call her his niece because she was the only niece he had.

Catherine rushed to him sobbing, she didn't know why, because really she was so happy to see him again, not dead but alive, her own dear uncle Con, whom she had loved since the first time she met him, when he had so kindly taken her by the hand as she stood paralysed with shyness in the crowded palace room, at the summons of the formidable old Grand Duke Edmond, her foreign grandfather. It all came back when she saw Con lying there, looking so haggard and grey, with a scrub of two days' beard and bruises on his cheek. But he was there! He wasn't dead!

She sat on the floor, leaning her head against Con's shoulder, while people came and went round him. Jeanne brought him some hot clear broth.

"Those charcoal burners!" she said. "The greasy stuff they gave him! Of course he couldn't take it."

Presently Rafael came in again, looking worried. "I can't find Giles. His door was still locked but he was gone. I think he must have climbed out of the window, which was open. But he has not taken his fishing things. Have you seen him, Catherine? Christie?"

But neither of the girls had seen Giles all day.

"Now we have to search again, for Giles!" said Raf, pushing his hand through his hair till it stood even more on end than usual. "This is naughty of Giles."

He went into the hall and sent some men to look down by the river and in the village. It was still daylight, though the sun was descending and the light reddening at the horizon.

At supper time, when they lit the lamps indoors, though outside the air was still full of soft light, Giles had not been found, but Max came into the dining room to say that Albert from the station, whom he had met at the inn, had seen Giles boarding the afternoon train to Felsenbourg.

"Felsenbourg? Why should he go there?" said Rafael, puzzled. "I should have thought he would have gone to Brussels, to his parents, if he was angry with me for shutting him up."

Nobody could make anything of it. But Paul said to Catherine, "You don't think he would go to Duke Julius, do you? He seems to admire him."

"But he hardly knows him well enough to go and stay," said Catherine.

Rafael glanced at the clock. "Well, there's no other train that stops at Xandeln tonight," he said. "I'll send someone by the early train tomorrow to look for him. I hope he will have the sense to go to Alphonse at the Angel, for the night."

They went back to the sitting room where Con was still lying on the sofa. He was not asleep, for he opened his eyes when they came in.

Raf sat down on a chair beside him. "What can you remember of all this, Con?" he asked.

"Nothing much, except that there was an almighty bang," said Con. "I've an idea I was creeping up a hill for hours, I can't think why. Was it a dream? And trying to get out of a mill race." He gazed at Rafael. "Where's Yolande?" he asked suddenly.

"She has gone to Nordwick with the baby," Rafael said. "And I want to send you there tomorrow, if you can stand the journey."

"To Nordwick? Why?"

"Julius has declared himself Grand Duke," said Rafael. "He thinks you were killed by that bomb and I'm afraid that if he finds you are alive, he won't exactly welcome the news."

"Good heavens," said Con, in such mild surprise that Raf smiled.

"Don't worry about it, but I thought I'd warn you," he said "Ah, here's Dr. Karelius. Clear out, everybody, please."

The Doctor was well known at the castle, since what with the cripples, the sick priests, the fugitives and the children, his services were often in demand.

They went into the hall where presently Rafael joined them. "Nothing much wrong with old Con, thank God," he said cheerfully. "He really is as tough as an old warhorse!"

The clock over the stables chimed three-quarters; it was a quarter to nine.

"Bedtime, and more than bedtime, for Toby and all persons under the age of ten," said Raf, rubbing the little boy's curly head, resting against him as he leaned against the heavy table, half sitting on it.

Just as Toby was protesting against this edict one of

the men who had gone out to look for Giles came running up the steps and rushed into the hall.

"Seigneur! Soldiers are coming!" he said breathlessly. "On the road from Felsenbourg. But a lot of soldiers! Medlerne men of Varenshalt's Hussars."

Rafael slid off the table. "Are you sure they are coming here?"

"Yes, because they are already approaching the bridge. What can it be, Seigneur? An attack? They are coming armed, we could see that."

Rafael said, "Medlerners! Can it be Julius? But how could he know?"

He stood for a moment, hesitating. Then he said, "We can't risk it. Con must go now—at once. He must go by the ferry and the moor road. They can get horses from the farm beyond Claus's cottage."

The doctor came out of the sitting room. Rafael turned to him. "Karelius! You must go at once with the Grand Duke to Nordwick. Go back to him now, please, and help him out here. Paul! Go down to the ferry stage and call Claus over. Tell him that when he has taken the Grand Duke across he must sink the boat on the other side and stay in his cottage. Max! Where's Max?"

"Here, Seigneur." Max appeared at his elbow.

"Max, have we some of that dynamite left that we used in the quarry?"

"Yes, in the shed half way down to the footbridge."

"Right. Take someone else with you and go and blow up the footbridge."

Max went straight away; Paul had already gone.

The doctor came out again with Con, who was

looking bewildered, holding his arm and limping a little. "Raf, what's happening?" he said. "I don't understand this. If the army is against me—"

"It's not the whole army," Raf interrupted him. "It's Julius's men and maybe Julius himself. You must go at once, Con. There's no two ways about it."

He turned round and shouted to the servants to bolt all the doors and close the shutters, all except those in the front of the house. "Leave them till last," he said. "We don't want them to think us prepared."

Everybody seemed to be set in motion by his orders, hurrying this way and that. Catherine and Toby both stayed where they were, silent and staring.

"Jeanne, the children? They're not all in bed yet?" Raf said. "Bring down the ones who are still up and dressed."

Jeanne ran up the stairs, turning to lean over the banisters and call out, "Raf! You don't go with Con?"

"Of course not," he answered.

Con, who was being piloted towards the kitchen door, stopped. "Raf, if there's going to be trouble here, I can't go and leave you, like this."

"There'll be worse trouble if you stay," Rafael said. "If you're not here, what can Julius do? If it is Julius. All this may be for nothing."

But at that moment another figure climbed panting up the castle steps. It was Albert, the porter from the station.

"Seigneur, it's Duke Julius himself who's coming, like he did before, but with many more soldiers. He's in the village now—at least, he's on the bridge."

Con made another attempt to refuse to leave but

Rafael went over and took his other arm and maneuvered him out of the door.

"You can send Gabriel, if you like!" Catherine heard him say.

The next moment Con was out of sight and Rafael shut the kitchen door and came back into the hall. Jeanne was coming downstairs with the orphan children.

"Raf! There'll never be time for him to get away," she said, white-faced.

"We'll have to make time for him," he said. "Julius will expect to surprise us—why else should he come at this hour? Somehow he must have heard something about Con, or suspect that he is not dead. We shall see in a moment. But whatever he wants, we must keep him here till Con's safely away."

As the children, goggle-eyed, crowded down into the hall, Raf went towards them and clapped his hands. "Listen, *mes enfants!* There's going to be a game of hide and seek. Some soldiers are coming and perhaps they will ask you where someone is hiding. But you must say, 'We don't know where he is! We haven't seen him!' Say it, whenever they ask you. Say it now."

And when they shouted in chorus he cried, "Very good! Don't forget now! 'We don't know where he is!'"

"We haven't seen him!" shouted the children, all together.

"But this will make them suspect that he is here," Jeanne said anxiously.

"Exactly!" said Raf, with a smile. Practically his entire household had now assembled in the hall. "Now, whatever these people want, we are anxious they should not find it," he said to them. "So nobody knows anything, not the simplest thing, such as where keys are kept. We are all dolts, at Xandeln, you understand?"

"Seigneur," said Nicolas the butler. "I can see the torches of those soldiers coming up the road."

"Right! Now we see them for the first time," said Rafael. "Quickly, the shutters for the lower windows. As they come through the gates, shut the great doors and bolt them."

He began to climb the stairs.

"Raf! Where are you going?" Jeanne said, bewildered.

"Just to the window up here so that I can talk to Cousin Julius," said Raf. He went along the gallery of the landing and stationed himself at the window above the front doors.

Catherine and Christie and Toby immediately ran up after him. Jeanne stayed downstairs with the children.

Looking out of the window from behind Rafael, Catherine saw soldiers riding through the gate and fanning out round the steps, as the great doors crashed together.

After a few moments Julius Varenshalt appeared, riding a fine grey horse. He was in his Hussar's uniform and attended by several officers. He could be seen quite clearly in the light of the torches. When they saw the castle doors close, the party halted.

Rafael pushed the tall casement window wide open.

"Well, Cousin Julius!" he called out. "This is not a very convenient time to come visiting Xandeln!"

10

No Escape

JULIUS VARENSHALT sat on his grey horse and looked up at the window where Rafael was standing.

"What have you done with Constant Waldemar?" he demanded.

"His body has not been found," replied Rafael.

"His body! I know that Constant is alive," said Julius impatiently.

"In that case I suppose you have given up your recently acquired title of Grand Duke," said Rafael, ironically.

"That is another matter," Julius said. "I was asked to take this office for the sake of our country and it is not to be repudiated just because my cousin is alive. You know well that his father did not consider him fit to succeed, that he declared him deprived of all his rights. Some of us feel that in the last year and a half he has proved his father only too right."

"I am not one of those critics of Constant," said Rafael. "As far as I am concerned he is still the Grand Duke and therefore I do not propose to give him up now to an usurper."

"So!" said Julius angrily. "You think you can keep me out of this house? Open the doors at once, or my men will break in."

"I don't think they will find it so easy," said Rafael, coolly.

Julius gave orders to his men and they moved to surround the house. Of course they then discovered that all the doors and windows were bolted and barred and shuttered against them. Presently the sergeant reported back that in order to break into the house they would have to bring up equipment.

"Blow this door down!" said Julius, annoyed. He looked up again at the window. "Open it, or we shall blast it open."

"I prefer you to have the trouble of opening it," said Rafael. He moved away from the window and back to the top of the stairs. "Nicolas!" he called. "Be ready to open the door when I tell you. We may as well let them waste as much time as possible."

Then he went back and watched the preparations to blow in the thick old doors. It took quite a time, and not until a soldier was almost ready to light the fuse did Rafael give the order to open them. He came down the stairs and went to the entrance, telling the children to stand back by Jeanne. When the doors were opened he walked to the threshold and called out, "I suppose you had better come in, Julius. Would you mind removing all this gunpowder?"

It was not surprising, Catherine thought, that Julius was already angry when he strode into the hall of Xandeln, following soldiers with drawn sabres who entered first, pushing Rafael aside without ceremony. He went over to one of the long tables and leant against it, with his stick in his hand.

"Aren't we going to fight them, Raf?" said Toby, belligerently.

"No, Toby," said Rafael. "You don't fight swords and guns with fists. Other ways, perhaps."

When Julius came in he looked all round, as if he had expected to see Constant Waldemar among the assembled company.

"Where is he?" he demanded.

"My dear Julius, you don't suppose I shall hand him over to you, the usurper of his right?" said Rafael. "If you want him, you must find him."

"Why should you suppose I mean him any harm?" Julius said. "Unless you yourself mean to use him for your own purposes, which I can well believe."

"What you believe, Julius, has always been a mystery to me," said Rafael. "It appears to rest on no foundation but your own wishes."

Julius said abruptly, "We shall search the house."

He turned away and gave his orders. Detachments of soldiers began a systematic search, while the household were ordered to remain in the hall, under guard. Soldiers with pistols and sabres stood at all the doors and Julius told two to watch Rafael. He himself, with Anton d'Hautrec and another officer, began to look into the rooms which opened off the hall. In the sitting room, where Con had so recently been lying on the couch, he immediately noticed that someone had been there—the blanket tossed aside and muddy marks on the cover and the carpet.

"You have had Constant in that room!" he accused Rafael, coming back into the hall.

"I never said we had not," said Rafael. "Yes, he was there not long ago. But now he is somewhere else." He pulled himself up on to the table, sitting on it, with his feet on the bench.

Toby scrambled up and stood on the table beside him, excited by the scene which he did not quite understand.

Then Julius's aide called to him and he went back into the sitting room.

As Catherine stood by the table she suddenly caught sight of Giles on the threshold, looking in. "Giles!" She went over to him. "Did you come with Duke Julius?" And then, suddenly guessing: "You didn't *tell* him?"

Giles reddened but he said, "Yes, I did. I thought he ought to know."

"But how did you know yourself? You were shut in your room when Raf told us."

"I heard him telling Paul no one must know Con was alive. I thought it was very suspicious behaviour," said Giles defiantly.

Catherine gazed at him in horror. "You suspected *Rafael?*" she said, incredulous. "And told *Julius?* Oh, Giles how could you?"

She ran across to where Raf was sitting on the table. "Raf, it was Giles who fetched Julius here," she said, nearly in tears.

Rafael glanced across at Giles. "Yes, I guessed that," he said quietly. "Giles has always suspected my motives ever since he saw me take your pocket money in

Trier." As he mentioned Trier, she saw his face change. "My God! I've forgotten Luca!" he whispered. "If they find him, it could be worse for him than for Con."

It was a dreadful moment. The men were already searching the house. There was no possibility of spiriting the Italians out of it now.

Then Rafael's eye fell on Christie Wilkin, sitting on the bench near his feet. He leant forward. "Christie, will you help me to save Luca?" he said. "I think he's told you about our escape from Venice, how we had to be French and then had to be German, to deceive the Austrians? Well, now I want you to go and make it seem he is English. His English speaking is much better than mine. Will you go and explain to him what is happening, and if any soldiers come in, play at being all my English visitors?"

"Of course I will," said Christie readily. "But I don't know the place where they are living here."

"I know!" cried Toby.

"That's it, Toby knows," said Raf. "Toby knows this game too, don't you, Toby? Remember those Austrian officers, how I pretended to be a German artist? Now, go with Christie and help Luca to pretend being English."

Toby jumped down from the table willingly. He loved acting and liked to feel he knew more than the older children, whether about the Italians or about escaping from enemies who spoke another language. He took Christie's hand and the two children went off towards the back of the hall. Julius was still in the sitting room.

A soldier tried to bar them from going out but when

Rafael called out something in dialect, he laughed and let them go through.

"What did you say?" Catherine asked.

"Can't you guess?" said Rafael with a smile. Then he took Catherine's hand and talked seriously to her.

"Catherine, my dear, I didn't ask you to play that game, because you are not just English, you are one of us too. In fact, I almost sent you with Con, for fear Julius might try to make use of you again, in his dynastic ambitions. But it seemed to me that by calling himself Grand Duke he had shown that he would ignore you. I hope I am right."

Then Catherine told him how Julius had questioned her aunt about marriage plans for her, and he laughed. "I can imagine your aunt Eleanor's face!" he said. "But evidently Julius is assured that they do not consider your claims here as important."

The search was still going on when a dull detonation shook the air.

Julius came out of the sitting room. "What was that?" he demanded of Rafael.

"How should I know?" said Raf. "Late blasting at the quarry? Or perhaps another revolutionary bomb?"

In fact, as Catherine guessed, it must be Max blowing up the footbridge. Not long after she saw Paul and Max come in at the front door; the soldiers did not stop anyone who was a member of the household coming in, only going out. Paul did not go straight to Rafael, but after a few minutes he sidled up to the table and leant on it near him to say quietly in English, "It's all right, Raf. Everything's gone according to plan."

"Well, that's a good start," said Raf. "Why didn't you go with them?"

Paul gazed at him in surprise. "But of course I came back to you," he said.

Rafael said nothing and Catherine suddenly realized that he did not know what would be the consequence of thwarting Julius, but expected it to be serious. She vividly remembered what had happened before, and anxiety seemed to twist and squeeze her inside. She saw Giles could not have realized what his act might lead to, but still it was difficult, for the moment, not to hate the sight of him.

Julius had not noticed Paul's entrance; he was now questioning the orphans, who were sitting at the other long table with Jeanne and Thérèse Brac.

"Have you seen the Grand Duke, who was blown up by assassins?" he asked.

"We don't know where he is!" chanted the children, delighted to say the piece Rafael had taught them. "We haven't seen him!" It sounded most unconvincing, although in fact it was perfectly true.

Raf smiled, and just as he did Julius turned round and saw him smiling. "So! You have been teaching these children what to say!" he said angrily.

"But it's true, isn't it, *mes enfants?*" said Raf. "You don't know where he is!"

"We haven't seen him!" they chanted back, several of the smaller ones jumping up and down with excitement.

"It's really time for them to go to bed, Julius," said Rafael. "Would you allow Madame Brac to go up and put them to bed?"

Julius, seeing that the children would be no use to him, did allow this.

"*Bonsoir*, Jeanne! *Bonsoir*, Raf!" cried the children, as they went upstairs.

Jeanne came over to the other table and sat on the bench near Rafael, next to Catherine.

Julius was growing impatient as the search proceeded and Constant was not found. The soldiers too began to get irritated and the search became rougher—some panelling was smashed in, walls kicked, tapestry prodded with sabres. Catherine was nervously awaiting the arrest of the Italians, but time went on and they did not appear. She could only guess that if they had been found, Christie and Toby had convinced the Letzenstein soldiers of the Englishness of the party.

Julius, who had walked out of the hall to see what was happening, now came back in a furious rage of frustration. He strode up to where Rafael was still sitting on the table and said harshly, "You will show me where he is! At once!"

"How do you know Con didn't hide himself?" Raf replied. "He knows this house, and all its hiding places, as well as I do."

Julius seized a loaded pistol from the nearest soldier and thrust it against Rafael's chest. "Find him!" he shouted.

"All right, all right," Raf said. "Take that thing away. I can't get down in case you let it off."

Julius removed the pistol but kept it aimed at Raf, who slid to the floor and started off towards the stairs. He did not go up them but opened a door underneath which led to some wooden steps going down. None of the soldiers had discovered this door, which was concealed in the panelling.

Raf disappeared down the steps, with Julius and some soldiers following; everyone else stayed in the hall.

"Whatever is he doing now?" Catherine wondered.

Jeanne said, in her halting English, "I fear for him, Catherine. He makes Julius very angry, doing like dis."

It was too true. When some time later Rafael led him back into the hall from the kitchens, after a prolonged ramble in the cellars, Julius was white with resentment.

"Well, I don't know," Raf was saying, "He *could* have been there."

A hatchet-faced man, whom Paul knew as Colonel Stenken, once head of the Special Corps which Con had disbanded after their illegal interrogation of Rafael in 1848, went up and spoke to Julius. After listening to him Julius turned on Raf. "Stenken thinks Waldemar is not here at all," he said. "That you have been playing tricks on us all this time."

"Stenken is always full of bright ideas," said Rafael. "There's nothing for it, is there, except to make sure whether he is here or not?"

"Very well," said Julius. "If you don't tell me the truth I shall burn this house down. The people must be taken outside and then we shall burn the castle, and if Constant is here, so such the worse for him."

"So you would burn your cousin the Grand Duke, would you?" said Rafael, with an edge of contempt in his voice. "Well, Julius, I am glad you cannot do that. I must admit that Stenken is right this time. Con is not here, so you may save yourself the trouble of burning Xandeln."

Julius glared at him, still uncertain whether to believe him or not. Catherine could well understand his doubt; Raf might be saying this simply to prevent Con's being burnt in the proposed holocaust.

They were standing in the middle of the hall. The clock outside chimed and struck eleven. It was two hours since Con had been hurried away from the castle.

Julius said, "If you want to convince me that he is not here, you had better tell me where he is."

"Well, I hope he is over half way to Nordwick by now," said Rafael calmly.

Julius stared at him for a moment and then hit at him with the first thing that came to hand, the butt of the pistol.

But Raf, who had been watching him closely, saw the blow coming and ducked his head. Julius nearly lost his balance, the pistol flew from his hand and hit the stone floor, but luckily did not go off. Several of the Xandeln men laughed.

Still further incensed, Julius said, "You'll be sorry for this." He turned to give orders to his men. He knew the district, though not well, and ordered them down to the ferry. Rafael said nothing to stop them, so more time was wasted while the soldiers went all the way down the hill, discovered that there was no boat, went round to the footbridge and found that it was blown up. They had to go back and report that the only way would be across Xandeln bridge and along the main road right up to Tiepol near the frontier, where there was another bridge.

Rafael had sat down again, in his own chair at the top of one of the tables. He leant his chin on his fists with an expression of detached interest, as if he had nothing to do with this collapse of communications.

Julius realized that he was beaten. It was now impossible to overtake Constant before he was in Nordwick territory and under the protection of the formidable Altenbergs. Stenken and Anton d'Hautrec both made that quite clear to him. The three of them stood near the big empty fireplace, where the chimney piece was carved with the le Marre phoenix on his pyre of flames, and discussed the situation. They were soon joined by Anton's father, Baron d'Hautrec, who had come in some time earlier and had been sitting near Giles, observing the scene.

Rafael called Catherine to him. "Catherine, you should go to bed now. The game is played out, you see." He looked tired, suddenly.

Catherine had an uneasy feeling that it was not played out; she felt that Rafael did not think so either and only wanted to get her out of the way before anything else happened. And Jeanne's face was tense with anxiety.

"Please need I?" she whispered. "I couldn't sleep, you know."

"Well, just go up and see if Christie is in your room, and what has happened about that part of the hide and seek," said Raf.

Catherine was willing enough to be useful. Nobody stopped her going upstairs.

Christie was sitting on her bed, but still dressed. She jumped up when Catherine came in. "Oh, Catherine, what's happening? I didn't dare come down for fear someone would ask me where I'd been."

Catherine told her that Julius had now discovered that Con was well on his way to Nordwick and that it was too late to overtake him.

"Then we've won! How marvellous!" Christie bounced excitedly on her bed, in triumph.

"But I'm sure Julius isn't going to give up," said Catherine. "He *can't,* if he means to stay Grand Duke." Then she asked about the Italians.

"Luca was tremendously English!" Christie said, giggling. " 'British Museum', he said. He put on some big spectacles and a smoking jacket Raf had lent him, and sat over some enormous books, making notes in English. When the soldiers came in, he looked at them over his glasses and said, 'What's this all about?' Almost like your diplomatic uncle, Catherine."

"And Silvia and Gaetano?"

"Well, they're both rather fair, as you know. They were singing and playing at the piano, a *French* song, and didn't say anything. Toby and I talked like mad, and I talked to the soldiers in English, which of course they couldn't understand, and then Luca said in French we were English friends of Raf's, and he tried to make his French sound like Englishmen's French. Anyway, the soldiers gave up and went away."

"Where's Toby?" asked Catherine.

"Silvia took him along to Madame Brac, though he wanted to go down and find Raf, as he always does."

When Catherine went out on to the landing to go and report this to Rafael, Christie came with her. They looked over, down into the hall.

Baron d'Hautrec was sitting with Julius at the other end of the long table from Rafael, and Julius was writing a letter. Anton d'Hautrec was lounging near Raf, pistol in hand, evidently considering that the two soldiers watching him were not enough security against his making an escape. Colonel Stenken was lining up the men of the household and as the girls watched, a squad of soldiers marched them out through the great doors.

"Oh, what's going to happen to them?" Catherine gasped. She ran down the stairs and across to Raf, repeating her question to him.

"They're going to be locked up in the village gaol," he answered. "Julius, or more probably Stenken, has realized that some of them have been quite busy tonight, doing what I asked them to do. So they feel safer without my men here, you see."

At that moment Julius signed his name to his letter with a flourish and called out to Anton d'Hautrec, "Right! Make him come here."

"Come on, le Marre," Anton said, nudging Raf with his pistol. "The Grand Duke wishes to speak to you."

"The Grand Duke is in Nordwick," said Rafael obstinately.

"Will you move?" said the young officer angrily.

Rafael got up slowly. "Paul, where's my stick?" he asked.

Paul ran to pick it up from the bench where he had left it but Anton d'Hautrec said, "No, no! No weapons, I say."

Raf laughed and walked down the room without it, rather stiffly and unevenly, and stood looking at Julius, who sat in a chair, reading through the letter he had just written.

"Now, le Marre," he said, "since this concerns you, although it is addressed to Constant Waldemar, I propose to read it to you." And he read, loud enough for everyone in the hall to hear:

"*Sir, my cousin:*

I have been informed that the bomb which was said to have killed you did not in fact do so. While I am glad to hear that you have escaped with your life, I wish to make it clear that the situation in Letzenstein has changed. On Wednesday last I was formally asked in the Chamber of Deputies to take over the duties of Grand Duke, since everyone was agreed that in a grave crisis like the present emergency the supreme power could not lie with a child, nor be safely invested in the regency which you designed. The supposed fact of your death gave occasion for this transfer of responsibility but I must beg to inform you that the news of your safety will not reverse the decision. The late Grand Duke, your father, declared you unfit for this office and after your eighteen months' rule we are convinced of your incapacity. I append a list of those who have given their assent to the transfer of power to me.

"I therefore wish you to leave Letzenstein the day you receive this letter, Friday, September 7th, and to sign the instrument of abdication which I enclose, in the presence of witnesses who are known members of a foreign government. You will renounce your claim and the claim of your son or other children, to the Grand Duchy, and will agree to live outside it for the rest of your life.

"Since you may imagine it possible to contend for the title, a contention which I should resist with arms, I wish to make

it clear to you that unless I receive this instrument of your abdication before midnight on Sunday, September 9th, your cousin Rafael le Marre will face summary execution for his activities in opposition to the government.

"I have enclosed two copies for your signature, one to be sent to Felsenbourg and one to Xandeln. If I receive it in time, Rafael le Marre's sentence will be commuted to exile for life.

Your cousin,
Julius, Grand Duke of Letzenstein."

Julius was evidently pleased with this epistle. He looked at Rafael to see how he took this sudden threat to his life.

Rafael turned to Baron d'Hautrec. "Very well expressed, Hautrec," he said, to Julius's annoyance. "But of course it is treason."

Jeanne, who had come up beside Rafael, now said, "But listen! This is not justice! How can you sentence him, either to exile or to execution, and without a court, just for assisting the one who is by right and law the Grand Duke? This is not possible!"

"It is quite possible, madame," said Baron d'Hautrec suavely. "The charge, as it will be reported in Felsenbourg, will be on account of complicity in the revolutionary activities which led to the bomb outrage. We know he knew Armand Grignol, one of the suspects. Execution would be carried out under the martial law now obtaining."

Jeanne was speechless with indignation and fear; she moved close to Rafael, taking his arm.

Raf said, "Justice has never been one of the Baron's interests, Jeanne. Order is what he prefers: his own order, of course." Then he said to Julius, "How do you propose to send this letter to Constant by Friday? It's nearly Friday now."

"I shall send it by special messenger at once," said Julius. "With an escort of guards." And he sneered, "You need not be afraid that he will not get it in time to save your skin."

"I thought I might write to him too," said Rafael mildly.

Julius gazed at him suspiciously. "To say what?" he demanded.

"Why should I tell you?" replied Rafael. "Never mind; someone else can take my letter later."

"You are not going to be in a position to write or send letters, le Marre," said Julius harshly.

"Oh Julius! You are not going to put me in the cellars *again?*" Raf mocked him. "This time, would you leave the wine there too, please?"

Julius jumped to his feet. "No!" he shouted furiously. "I am not going to put you in the cellars! I am going to keep you here where you can be seen. Believe me, there will be no escape for you this time."

He spoke to Stenken who gave an order in dialect to the soldiers. Julius's solution to the problem of preventing Rafael from escaping was to handcuff him to two men, one each side. To do this, they had to ask Jeanne to step aside.

"Courage, Jeanne," whispered Raf, kissing the side of her face before she moved. "We are not finished yet."

The children had all heard him say this before, in moments of danger, but somehow it was hard to believe that this was not the end. Either Rafael would have to leave Xandeln forever, or he would be executed.

"Colonel Stenken is in command of this castle," announced Julius to everyone left in the hall. "Remember that Letzenstein is at present under martial law. Serious disobedience will be punished with death. You are forbidden to take orders from Rafael le Marre. Colonel Stenken will give you your orders. Now we shall shut the doors and retire for the night."

"You had better sleep in the room Sir Walter had, Julius," said Rafael. "There isn't much space here just now, so perhaps Anton would not mind sharing with you."

Christie giggled, she could not help it, because Rafael somehow always managed to spoil the effect of Julius's speeches by bringing things down to an everyday level.

But she wished she had not when Julius, irritated beyond his limited powers of control, turned and hit Rafael hard in the face with his fist, so that he staggered back against the table, falling sideways over it, unable to save himself because his arms were held by the handcuffs to the soldiers.

Catherine gasped, Christie cried out and Paul made a dive forward but was caught and pulled back by Anton d'Hautrec.

And Jeanne shouted in Julius's face, "You coward! You bully!"

He retorted, insultingly, "That fishwife style quite suits you, madame." And then he ordered her, and everyone else, out of the hall.

So they had to go upstairs and leave Rafael there.

They saw him sit down on the bench and try to wipe the blood from his face, for his nose was bleeding. He waved to them, with a chained hand, as they went upstairs, but that made Catherine cry.

"No escape, this time," she kept saying to herself, as she climbed wearily into bed.

11

Storms Threatening

CATHERINE WOKE in sunlight and for a moment she could not think why she felt engulfed in a grey cloud. Then she remembered last night, and Julius's ultimatum to Constant, which threatened Rafael's life. Conscious unhappiness succeeded her first unrecognized unease. Christie was still asleep, her curly yellow head pressed into her pillow, one arm flung out over the covers. Catherine dressed quietly and went downstairs.

As she descended she saw Raf coming into the hall, still handcuffed each side to a soldier, but they were different soldiers. He looked untidy, unshaven and tired, as if he had not slept very much.

Jeanne was at one of the long tables serving out breakfast to the orphans. When she saw Rafael she went across to him and Catherine could hear them talking in French. Then the soldiers took Raf over to the other table and made him sit down on the further side of it. Jeanne brought him a cup of coffee.

By this time Catherine had reached the bottom of the stairs and Jeanne called to her to come and have breakfast with the orphans.

"Unless you want to have it with Julius and his friends in the dining room!" said Paul.

Catherine slid into the bench beside Paul. She had hardly begun eating when the dining room door opened and Julius came out, with Baron d'Hautrec. The Baron had come in his carriage the evening before and Julius was going back with him to Felsenbourg. He stood in the middle of the hall, giving final orders to Colonel Stenken. Hanging about in the doorway behind was Giles.

At last Julius was ready to leave. He turned towards Rafael and the two guards immediately rose and stood to attention. Raf remained sitting.

"Stand up, when the Grand Duke wishes to speak to you," said Stenken, sharply.

"One doesn't stand up for usurpers," said Raf, and drank his coffee.

But the soldiers pulled him to his feet.

"You have three days, le Marre," said Julius. "But I shall certainly see you again before they are up."

"Something to look forward to, you think?" said Raf, ironically.

Julius reddened. Rafael could always annoy him so easily. However, this morning he was confident of the success of Baron d'Hautrec's ultimatum; whichever way things turned out, he would get rid of one of his enemies.

"I warn you," he said, "if you try to escape, you will be shot. And if anyone of your people tries to leave Xandeln, you will be held responsible. I include the English children staying here. Every person is to remain till I return. No one is to leave the castle. If anyone disappears, it is you who will suffer, le Marre. So, I advise you to play no more tricks."

Rafael did not reply. He picked up his cup and drank the last of his coffee.

Julius was irritated, but he said no more. He went out of the hall and down the steps into the forecourt, the Baron and his son following. Rafael immediately sat down again and began to eat the croissant Jeanne had given him.

"Are we all right for stores, Jeanne?" he called across to her. "Enough till Monday?"

"Oh yes," she replied, but her voice was a little unsteady as she heard him name that fatal day so casually. "We have fewer to feed, without all the men. Unless we have to feed the soldiers too?"

"What do you say to that, Stenken?" said Rafael, rather as if the Colonel were an unexpected guest. "Do you feed us, or do we feed you?"

"I want no advice from you," said Stenken coldly. "Understand that you are no longer master here, but a prisoner."

He had a difficult task on his hands, for Julius had told him not to let Rafael le Marre out of his sight, and therefore Stenken could not altogether prevent him talking to other people present, though he tried to stop them talking to him. He quickly silenced the two guards, to whom Rafael had been talking till then quite freely. They were forbidden to answer him. But Stenken did not take much notice of the children. Toby, as soon as he had finished his breakfast, ran over to the other table and began playing with a little wooden engine which Max had made for him, running it along imaginary railway lines, with much puffing. Raf made a turntable of his saucer, much to Toby's delight.

Christie came down very late and Rafael immediately sent Toby across to fetch her.

"Christie, my dear," he said in English, which he knew was an unknown tongue to Stenken as well as to the soldiers. "Will you continue to belong to our *English* friends in the summerhouse? Have your meals with them? But you can go on sleeping in Catherine's room. So, you can be our *liaison*. Will you do this? It is important to me."

"Yes, all right," she said, a little reluctantly. She looked at him and said in her frank way, "You look awful, Raf. Are you ill?"

"No, I'm just tired," he said. "They didn't include bed in my night. The guards were changed to get a rest, but I didn't get one."

Jeanne evidently understood this, for she said anxiously, "*Tu nas pas dormi,* Raf?"

"Oh yes, I can sleep without lying down," he said, speaking in French, as he always did to her.

That caught Stenken's attention and he interposed, forbidding Jeanne to talk to Rafael.

Catherine went with Christie to visit the Italians. She had not before seen what Raf called the summerhouse. It was a room with many windows built out into a spinney at the back of the castle, with a view over to the moors, and it had a bedroom above, up a spiral stair. It had been built for Lucien le Marre, Grand Duke Marius's cousin and Rafael's godfather, a pianist who had lived at Xandeln years ago.

They found Luca Caravelli very anxious about Rafael. "Should we not try to rescue him from these villainous men?" he said.

"I don't see how you could," said Catherine. "Duke Julius told Stenken to shoot him if anyone did anything, and he's watching all the time."

"Well, I will do my best to play the Englishman, unconcerned with the strange behaviour of these foreigners, since this is what Raf wants," said Luca, but he sighed as he went back to his books.

The two girls wandered back through the garden. They saw Giles hanging about, but when he caught sight of them he went indoors.

"He seems ashamed to meet us," said Catherine.

"Well! I should hope he is!" cried Christie.

Paul had said that Giles had not slept in their room. "And I'm glad he didn't. It's his fault we're in this mess. I don't want to speak to him."

But Giles did not give them a chance to avoid him. He avoided them.

It turned out an oppressively hot day. There was thunder building up and a bronze haze took the freshness from the air and shadowed the light without reducing the heat. After the midday meal, Colonel Stenken, irritated at having to endure Rafael's far from silent presence, sent him outside to walk round the gravel sweep with his guards. But Stenken sat near the open door, where he could see him. He was writing a report for Baron d'Hautrec, but he had his pistol on the table.

Presently Raf sent Toby for his hat. It was extremely hot outside and the heat rebounded from the gravel.

Even Toby got tired of following Raf round and ran away to lie in the shade. But whenever Raf tried to stop to rest, Stenken ordered the guards to move on. After an hour the guards were changed but time went on, and still Rafael was not recalled.

At last Jeanne went up to Stenken's table. "Colonel Stenken," she said. "Perhaps you don't realize that such a long exercise is bad for Monsieur le Marre because of his back injury. Please let him come in and rest now."

"Madame, it is I who give orders here now, not you," said Stenken rudely. "Le Marre appears to be unaware that he no longer has any authority in this place. He had better learn more suitable behaviour as soon as possible."

Jeanne did not know what to do. She looked at Catherine, who had come with her, and they went through the sitting room to the garden and stood at the corner, by Giles's magnolia tree, watching Raf's progress, which was getting slower and slower and more and more uneven. When he came round to where they were he stopped and smiled, but his face looked very pale under the shade of his big hat.

"When does this exercise end, do you know?" he said. "It seems long."

"Raf, he is doing this to make you realize he is master here, not you," said Jeanne.

"Oh, is he?" said Raf, standing up straighter. "Well! We'll see!"

A shout came from the doorway; Stenken was ordering the soldiers to go on.

Rafael turned half round and called out, "Stenken!

Why don't you come out too? Such a fine day. Don't be so lazy, sitting there all the afternoon!"

He went on, smiling.

"Oh Raf, you dear idiot!" Jeanne murmured to herself. "Why can't you behave like anyone else, just for once?"

Presently she moved round the corner. "Catherine, I just can't watch," she said. She sat down on the grass, leaning against the wall of the house, and closed her eyes, with a gesture not of fatigue but of pain. "How does one live through such a three days?" she whispered.

Catherine sat so that she could see them both, and glancing up once she saw that Giles was looking out of the window of Paul's room, above. He did not see her but was watching Rafael as he shuffled round the gravel sweep yet once more. The soldiers were red in the face and sweating with heat. Catherine noticed that one of them was helping Raf occasionally, supporting his arm instead of just walking beside him as the other did.

"I ought not to have said that," Jeanne remarked presently. "Now he will never give in. He's such a very obstinate person, Catherine." But her mouth shook as she said that.

Stenken shouted, "Have you had enough, le Marre? Do you want to come in now?"

"Just as you like," said Raf. "You give orders, not me!"

It was so like him to use Stenken's own words to defy him that even Jeanne had to smile. She looked round the corner and then began to scramble to her feet. "I think he's going to faint," she said, and ran across the hot gravel.

Raf would certainly have fallen if the soldiers had not held him up. He did not pass out but they had to help him up the steps into the house and his sitting down on the nearest bench was almost a collapse.

But if Stenken imagined he could prevent Rafael from being the centre of the household by reducing him to a state of physical weakness, he soon found out his mistake. Whatever he did to Rafael he could not alter the attitude of the other people in the castle, whose habit of referring to him was based not merely on his position as their Seigneur, but on personal trust.

As Paul knew from experience, Raf had a natural resilience which soon asserted itself when he was able to rest, and by Angelus time he seemed to have recovered from the exhaustion of the afternoon and was reading the Letzenstein newspaper, which had arrived on the evening train. There were large blanks in its columns, where certain reports had been censored. Paul, who had been helping one of the crippled boys to practice walking in another room, had come back and was sitting near Raf, on the other side of the table. He asked, in English, what the blanks meant.

"That our friend Baron d'Hautrec is back at the Ministry of the Interior," said Rafael. "I wonder if he is censoring the news that goes out of the country too? There's nothing here about Con's being found alive."

Presently the orphans came in for their supper, which they had earlier than the rest of the household. While they were at it the delayed thunderstorm finally broke;

the clouds which had banked up so slowly now discharged right over Xandeln.

Catherine went to the window to watch; she rather enjoyed the fearful splendours of thunderstorms. But some of the children were frightened. The two little Brac girls began to cry.

"Don't be frightened," Jeanne said. "It won't hurt you, Babette. It's just a big noise in the sky."

"Don't like that big noise," sobbed Babette.

A flash of lightning illuminated the valley outside with a pinkish glare. It seemed to envelop the castle in its weird electric power. Then a tremendous crack sounded right overhead and the reverberations thundered on for several seconds.

"You know what that is, *mes enfants?*" Raf said. "It's those giants in the sky moving their furniture about. Terribly clumsy brutes they are, always dropping things." Another crash sounded, and rumbles of thunder. "There! They've let the chest of drawers tumble downstairs!" Raf cried. "Listen! There goes another drawer! Things falling out all the way down!" A final crack split the air. "The bottom drawer! All the family albums in it, the giants' pictures in daguerreotype!"

Some of the children laughed and when the next rattle of thunder sounded, one of the boys said, "What's that, Raf?"

"Just a bit careless with the chairs," said Raf. "Trying to carry too many at once. But hey! Look out, there goes the wardrobe! Right down the stairs!" It certainly was the biggest crack of the storm, ending with a dull thump. "The drawer fell out," Raf said, making a face of mock concern.

For the children the thunderstorm had become a game, and they were arguing as to which pieces of furniture the giants were dropping now. They were almost disappointed as the thunder receded.

Rain was coming down now in grey sheets outside the windows. The valley disappeared. The gravel sweep, such a desert that afternoon, was covered with pools of water. Through the din of the storm Catherine could hear the church bells clanging in the village.

"Lucky the harvest is in," said Raf.

Colonel Stenken thought it best to ignore this domestic scene. Later, after the storm had muttered away into the distance and the orphans had gone to bed, another occurred which he could hardly ignore. An old woman came hurrying in from the kitchen, going straight to where Rafael was sitting and bursting into a stream of agitated complaint in the local dialect.

Presently Rafael called out in French, "Did you hear that, Stenken? She says some of your men, off duty, have made themselves drunk on our wine and are terrorizing the girls in the kitchen. I think you had better do something about it, since you are in command here."

Stenken said, "She should have come to me, not you."

"Of course, of course," said Rafael soothingly. "But it is me she knows, you see."

Stenken did not reply, but he sent his second-in-command to deal with the drunken soldiers.

The last thing that happened that evening was that Jo-jo, the young priest with the bad heart, came to consult Rafael about the mass next day. Although it was only a Saturday, it was the feast of the Blessed Virgin's nativity and, Jeanne told Catherine, the anniversary of the reconsecration of the old chapel of the castle, after it was wrecked by the French in the revolutionary wars more than fifty years ago.

"It was a birthday present to Nôtre Dame," Jeanne said.

"But we don't know when her birthday was," said Catherine.

"But she must have had one!" said Jeanne.

So next morning there was mass in the chapel which nearly all the castle people attended. Round the walls, in brackets at the consecration crosses, candles were burning. Monsieur Jo-jo said the mass and when he had given communion to everyone at the altar rails he walked down to the back, where Rafael was standing with his guards, and gave it to him.

Candles in the morning light: Catherine thought how many people had found refuge at Xandeln during the last year, and her heart ached. Monday would see the end of it all, whatever happened.

When they went back into the hall, Giles was there, reading a letter. As Rafael passed him, he said in English, "Giles, will you come, please? Catherine too."

He and the soldiers sat down on one side of the table and Catherine on the other. Giles came up slowly, the letter in his hand.

"Is it from Sir Walter?" Rafael asked. "Does he know what is happening in Letzenstein?"

"He hadn't heard the news when he wrote," said Giles. "Perhaps he has now."

"Listen, Giles," said Rafael seriously. "I want you and Catherine and Miss Lacey to travel to Brussels on Monday, or as soon as you can."

"Oh no, Raf!" Catherine implored him.

"A moment, Catherine," he said. He put his hand across the table and took hers, holding it. "Giles, I want you to apologize to your father for me. I had no idea, when he left, that you and Catherine would be put in danger like this. But I think Julius will let you go. He has no more wish than Sir Walter for an incident which would involve Her Majesty's government! So, will you do this, Giles, please?"

"All right," said Giles, reluctantly.

But somehow he could not just leave it at that. Ever since Thursday night he had been realizing how badly he had misjudged Rafael's intentions and his character. Julius's letter to Constant had shown him how much Rafael had risked in getting Con away from Xandeln— and what might have happened had he been found there, still in a weak and dazed state. Julius's own behaviour had made Giles see the ruthless ambition behind his conventional manner. Yesterday, the way the castle people still turned to Raf, although he was a prisoner, at last made Giles understand his true position in Letzenstein as Seigneur of Xandeln, for so long the ancestral castle of the le Marres. While Stenken's harshness and Raf's way of resisting him, forced Giles to revise his opinion of the sort of person he was. And now he knew that it was his fault that Rafael was living under the threat of exile or death.

Red in the face, Giles blurted out, "I wish I hadn't told Julius that Con was alive and you were hiding him!"

"Well! I too wish this, I admit!" said Rafael, with a smile. "But if you are sorry, Giles, I am glad of that. I don't like to be thought such a snake—was it? No, *sneak*—funny word!—such a sneak as to use Con for some political game of my own. Why did you think I would do that?"

But Giles was too miserable to explain his suspicions; they seemed stupid now and unjustifiable. "I wish I could do something to help you," he said. "Can't I?"

Rafael pondered. Then he said, "Yes. You could go down to the village and find out if my men are all right and what, if anything, the Mayor is doing. I don't think Stenken would stop *you*. But if he does, never mind."

Giles, relieved to get away and to have something to do, went off at once.

Catherine stayed. "Raf," she said, "please don't send me away on Monday."

"My dear child, I must," he said gravely. "If I am exiled, Jeanne and I will be leaving soon after. Or else, it may be that Sunday is my last day. I would send you now, except that we have to wait for Julius to return. Stenken will keep everyone here till then."

"Julius *can't* do such an awful thing," whispered Catherine, in anguish.

"Well, let's hope he can't," said Rafael in matter of fact tones. "It puzzles me, I must say, why Gabriel seems to be doing nothing. It is not like him."

Stenken suddenly came striding across the room.

"This conversation must stop," he said, speaking in

French. "Why are you always talking with these English children?"

"Because I am fond of them," said Rafael. He gave Catherine's hand a gentle squeeze before he let it go and added, "Remember the phoenix, Catherine, my dear." This was in English.

Colonel Stenken motioned to Catherine to follow him to his desk. She stood in front of him and he stared at her with his sharp light eyes. "What was that he said? Phoenix? What is this? Tell me in French."

In French then, Catherine said, "You must know that the phoenix is the le Marre crest. It is everywhere here." She pointed to the one carved on the chimney piece over the wide fireplace: the great phoenix with outspread wings and upraised curving beak, in his pyre of leaping flames. And she thought of the motto written on the scroll underneath: *Per ignem idem*—through fire the same.

"Why did he speak of it? Why now?" Stenken demanded.

"I think because it is a sign of the resurrection," said Catherine. "The phoenix rises again from his own ashes. He told me that, once."

"Oh, if that is all!" said Stenken, relaxing. He gave a wintry smile. "Fortunately le Marre is not himself a phoenix!"

He dismissed Catherine, who went out through the sitting room into the garden. She found her knees were shaky. It was frightening, being asked questions by Stenken. Paul was in the garden drawing and asked what was the matter. When she told him he was sympathetic.

"I know what you feel like," he said, "Because he and the Baron asked me questions like that in the Old Fort, hoping I should somehow give Raf away to them."

Catherine told him about Giles's apology. "Well, I'm glad he realizes what he's done," was all Paul could find to say about that.

Giles came back from the village full of news, which he told first to them, as he returned through the garden. "Max and another man have escaped from the gaol. The Xandeln Deputy has gone back to Felsenbourg to make known what's happening here—but only yesterday afternoon. The Mayor was going to come up here, but the thunderstorm washed that out—almost washed *him* out, his house was flooded."

It was reassuring to hear that the village was not inactive. Giles's biggest news, however, was that the Civil Guard had caught two men suspected of being implicated in the bomb outrage; the name of one was Armand Grignol. Catherine remembered the surly man Gaetano had introduced to Raf on the wharfside, who had taken the fiery young Italian to the Republican meeting. And Baron d'Hautrec had spoken of using his name against Rafael to justify, after the event, the proposed execution. The assassins had to be put in the village gaol too and had nearly been lynched by the men from the castle.

"The Mayor says he's never had so many men in gaol ever," said Giles. "And most of them good men, he said, not thieves."

The Mayor, with a deputation of village seniors, arrived at the castle that afternoon. For some time

Stenken kept them talking outside but then he allowed the Mayor and two others to come in. His purpose was to show them that Rafael was still alive and well, for they had expressed doubts of this. Though they were pleased to see him alive, the Mayor and his friends were far from agreeing that he looked well.

"Seigneur, these men are ill treating you?" the Mayor asked him. "You look ill—your face is bruised, surely?"

"It is mostly dirt," said Stenken scornfully.

"Well, how can one wash with a couple of men on one's hands?" said Raf, shaking his handcuffs and smiling. "Monsieur le Maire, I am very grateful for your call. I am sorry to tell you that these men are trying to use me as a kind of hostage to force the Grand Duke, Constant, to leave Letzenstein. You know he is at Nordwick, alive?"

"We heard a rumour—" began the Mayor, but Stenken interrupted harshly, "Enough of this! Be silent, le Marre!"

Rafael, having said what he wanted to say, shrugged his shoulders and made a gesture of yielding the point. Stenken marshalled the Mayor away.

Raf, who had found a black crayon in his pocket, amused himself drawing on the censored blanks of the newspaper. His caricature of Stenken made even the anxious Paul smile, and he saw the soldiers too thought it all too life-like. Raf did not talk to his guards only because Stenken punished them if they answered him. But he seemed to be able to make friends with them all the same. Now, one of them winked over his head at the other.

So that long Saturday wore on into evening. The air was still thundery and oppressive; the storm had not cleared the air because there was more to come.

As the sun was setting, turning the western haze to hot bronze, Catherine went into the garden and saw Jeanne, leaning on the wall alone, looking across the hills towards Nordwick. There were tears on her cheek.

Catherine shyly put her arm round her and kissed her.

"Oh, Catherine!" Jeanne said, hugging her. "Why don't we hear anything? We are so cut off! Why nothing from Nordwick? And I am afraid—because Raf, who never fears for anything to happen till it does happen—he seems to think that this time Julius will not let him go."

"But Julius would have to, if Con abdicated," Catherine said. Somehow she was counting on that. She cared more for the lives of those she loved than for who was the ruler of Letzenstein.

Jeanne shook her head. "When I said that very thing, Raf, he only replied so—'Shot while trying to escape.'"

"What did he mean?"

"That's what they say when they kill someone before they have got the legal process done," said Jeanne, who in her travelling, city life had learned more of lawlessness than law.

They were silent for some moments and then Jeanne said, "It is so tormenting, to have him there all the time but never to be alone for an instant. Everyone watching and listening. What do they think he will do?"

"Escape," said Catherine. "He always has, before."

She knew Paul was still desperately hoping that somehow Rafael would trick his guards and get away.

Jeanne said, "Once I refused to marry Raf—you know that, Catherine. I didn't want his life, I wanted my life, ambitious creature that I was, so stupid! I did not want to have to follow his life, always mixed up with Italian republican politics, as it was then. I knew nothing about his position here, but if I had, even less would I have consented to marry him. And yet—now! Now I just can't imagine living without him."

She looked at Catherine, with a sort of smile on lips that trembled. "It would be so *dull!*"

Catherine knew she did not mean this to comprehend the whole of her feelings, but it expressed something of the way their relationship had developed, almost, it seemed, to Jeanne's surprise.

Then Jeanne sighed and moved away from the wall, turning towards the house again.

"Well! Somehow this night must be endured," she said.

12

The Last Day

SUNDAY BEGAN AS usual with mass. Catherine went to the first, before breakfast, because Jeanne had told her Rafael was going to it. The old Canon was saying the mass; when Catherine came into the chapel he was hearing Rafael's confession. The confessional was the kind where the priest sat inside the box but the penitent knelt at the side, so that you could see at a glance there was someone there. For this rite Raf had been released from his guards, who were standing one each side of the doors at the back, inside the chapel, which was a freestanding building, next to the ruined part of the old castle. But his hands were handcuffed together behind his back. Stenken was taking no chances.

So Rafael was able to come and kneel at a prie-dieu next to Jeanne, in his accustomed place, for the mass. Catherine was on the other side of Jeanne and Paul next to Raf. Although Catherine kept thinking "Suppose this is the last time he's here with us?" she found herself drawn into the deep heart of the communion with Christ at his last supper as never before. This event, Christ's sacrifice of himself, was present in the world till the end of all things. And so very simply, through the signs of bread and wine, every person could enter into it and find life out of death.

Christ had said his peace was a special kind of peace and Catherine felt how true this was; there was peace in this communion which they all shared, even though the end of the day could, it seemed, bring only exile or death.

There had been thunder in the distance all night and as they went into the hall rain began to fall, and it continued heavily all the morning. Xandeln seemed folded in greyness, in cloud and mist and water.

Catherine presently went to the window on the half-landing, from which Rafael had spoken to Julius last Thursday—how long ago it seemed now! Paul came up behind her. He looked so very sad that she said, "Nothing else wrong, Paul?"

"No," he replied. "It's just that Raf has been telling me what he has decided about my guardianship if he —if he . . ." but he could not finish that sentence. "He knows I would hate to go back to my English relations, who are very narrow-minded people. He wants me to stay with Jeanne; and Con, if he is Grand Duke still, or Gabriel d'Altenberg to be the other guardian. He's thought it all out and written it down, when Stenken wasn't looking."

He showed her a piece of paper, written rather thickly with the black crayon Raf had found in his pocket.

"There's more too about Toby and finding his English relations," said Paul. "And he wants us to be sure to keep Toby away on Monday, if anything happens.

Oh, Catherine! Somehow it makes it seem inevitable, though he kept saying, 'It's only *in case* something happens.'"

"Paul," said Catherine, "why don't the people from the village rescue Raf, as they did in January '48?"

"Too many soldiers," said Paul. "Not only here but in the village, and all the men from the castle locked up. Besides, Stenken is always watching. Any move and he would find it a good excuse just to shoot Raf himself."

"Doesn't he ever go to bed? Stenken?" Catherine asked.

"Yes, but he leaves officers on duty then. You heard what Raf said—he's not allowed to go and lie down, so he spends the night here as well as the day. And even the guards are always changed one at a time."

They stared gloomily out into the rain. Three figures appeared at the gate, challenged by the guards there. But they were passed, and presently came across the wet gravel.

"It's Albert from the station," Catherine said, "and two Civil Guards."

"I wonder what he's come for?" said Paul, and both of them hurried down the stairs into the hall, reaching it at the same time as Albert, who came in, stamping his feet and shaking the rain from his cape. He took off his peaked cap and looked all round. Then he walked up to Raf and said, "Seigneur, news from Felsenbourg!"

"Address yourself to me," said Colonel Stenken in his harshest tone. "I am in command here."

Albert looked at him and then back at Rafael, hesitating.

"If you speak loud enough, Albert, we shall all hear," said Raf, with a smile. "But face him."

Albert cleared his throat. "We have news from our Deputy," he said, in the voice in which he announced the trains. "The Princess Yolande is in Valmay with her son and Valmay has declared against Duke Julius."

"Good for Yolande!" cried Raf and thumped the table with his fist in his delight.

"In Felsenbourg," continued Albert, well pleased with the effect he was creating, "the Deputies have met again in defiance of Duke Julius's wishes and Count Gilbert d'Altenberg has told them that Grand Duke Constant was not killed by the bomb but is alive, though he is ill."

"Con ill?" Raf said. "Badly ill?"

"We don't hear anything of this, Seigneur," Albert said. "Just that he is ill and that therefore the Princess and the Duke of Nordwick are acting for him at present."

"Is Gabriel in Felsenbourg, then?" Rafael asked.

"That we don't know either, but our Deputy thought he was in Valmay with the Princess," said Albert.

"Julius forgot Valmay," said Rafael. "It is only united to Letzenstein because of Yolande's marriage to Con."

Stenken here interrupted, ordered Rafael to be silent and called Albert over to be questioned. Albert went, making a gesture which graphically expressed his opinion of Stenken.

Everyone began talking of the news, even the soldiers. Raf was tremendously pleased. "I knew the Altenbergs would do something," he said. "But I never thought of Yolande. She's got spirit, that girl!"

"But Raf," said Jeanne anxiously, "won't Julius count this as a refusal of his ultimatum? It puts you more in danger than ever."

"A lot can happen before midnight," he said, as usual refusing to live in fear of the future. He took Jeanne's hand across the table, as he had taken Catherine's the day before, and smiled at her. "Julius may be too busy to execute me! To keep the power he has seized is more important to him than scoring off an old enemy." Then, still thinking of Albert's news, he added, "But poor Con! I expected too much even of his great strength, sending him on that night ride so soon after we found him. But what could one do? There was no time to think."

Giles was looking at the Civil Guards who had come with Albert. One of them looked very like Max. Could Max have a brother in the Civil Guard? They did not go away after their news was given but went to the kitchen for refreshments. This was Raf's suggestion but Stenken, preoccupied with what for him was bad news, did not notice or interfere.

Then it was time for the midday meal. The rain stopped. It was humid and grey outside, a soft windless air.

Stenken was restless in the afternoon and more than usually irritated with Rafael. He ordered the children away every time they approached him and at last seized a kicking and biting Toby and shouted at him, "I am going to shut you up in the cellar, you disobedient little ape!"

Toby howled. "No! No! Don't want to!"

"Don't shut him up," Raf said. "Stay with Jeanne, Toby. Be a good boy."

But Stenken pushed the child into the door under the stairs. He did not notice when some time later Toby, who was no fool, discovered the latch high up on the door and quietly let himself out.

But Paul saw him and quickly took him into the sitting room, which Stenken never used, probably because it was used so much by the family, going in and out to the garden.

Stenken, finding that Raf, sitting at the long table, was still a focal point for his household, made him move nearer himself. He had had a desk carried into the hall, from which he had a view both of the front door and the doors to the kitchen. He made Raf stand by this desk for the rest of the afternoon, so that anyone approaching him would have to talk under Stenken's immediate scrutiny. Nobody liked to do this.

The guards, as usual, were changed, but Rafael was left standing all the time.

Jeanne, watching him, said to Catherine, "I suppose if I say anything to Stenken it will only make it worse for Raf. Well! It isn't so bad for him as walking in the sun."

But standing for hours is tiring to anyone, and to Raf, with his injured back it was a considerable strain. As the hour of Angelus approached he was looking exhausted.

At that hour, quite without warning, Duke Julius arrived, in his own fast carriage, drawn by two pairs of horses. The Baron was not with him.

Julius came quickly up the steps into the castle. Stenken rose and saluted.

"Everything all right here, Stenken?" Julius said, giving a quick look round.

From his point of view everything was in order. Rafael was present and a prisoner; the situation at Xandeln was unchanged.

Catherine thought there was something tense in Julius's manner. She felt he was in a state of suppressed rage, but there seemed to be something of fear in it too. It must be the Princess's move, she decided. Valmay's defiance complicated everything, especially now that it was known that Constant was alive.

Julius took Stenken's arm and they walked up and down the middle of the hall, talking in low voices. Presently they went back to the desk and Julius stood behind it, Stenken beside him.

"Well, le Marre, I have had no answer from Constant Waldemar," said Julius.

"It's not midnight yet," Raf pointed out.

Julius smiled—the most hideous smile Catherine had ever seen, a kind of silent snarl or sneer.

"He has answered it negatively by sending the Princess to Valmay," he said. "Evidently the Baron overestimated the value Constant put on your life. When it comes to the point, he prefers his title to you."

"Constant has a duty to this country," said Rafael. "He is justified in putting it before personal considerations."

Julius regarded him in silence for a moment. Then he said, "I suppose you think I shall not carry out the threat that was made in that ultimatum?"

"My dear Julius, don't ask me to guess what goes on in your mind," said Rafael. "But whether or not you intend to execute me at midnight, for the present I am going to take the weight off my feet in a more pleasant way."

Before the guards realized what he was going to do he pulled the chair from behind Stenken, who was standing, and sat down on it.

"Stand up!" shouted Stenken, enraged.

"Can't," said Raf.

Julius intervened. "I have to leave before midnight," he said. "I do not propose to go before doing what I said I would do with you, Rafael le Marre."

Catherine heard Jeanne gasp. Suddenly the reality of the threat of the last three days was upon them.

Raf was looking intently at Julius with those very keen, very blue eyes of his.

"Something's happened in Felsenbourg," he said. "Have our Felsenburgers turned against you, Julius, now that they know Constant is alive? I think they won't take you for their Grand Duke after all. Are you, by any chance, on your way across the frontier now?"

Everybody in the room stared at Julius. Catherine heard Paul whispering, "I believe he's right; Raf's right. Julius has lost the game."

"Whatever has happened in Felsenbourg will make no difference to you, le Marre," said Julius at last. "Stenken, you have your orders."

Stenken stepped forward at once and rapped out orders in the Letzensteiner German, so that none of the children knew what he was saying. The soldiers on duty jumped to attention and marched outside. Julius went out too and down the steps. Raf's guards pulled him to his feet and took him out of the door, Stenken following with his pistol in his hand.

Terrified, Catherine and Paul and Giles were almost the first of the rest of the household to get over the threshold. The first of all was Jeanne, who was desperately trying to get to Raf, but was caught and held by two soldiers. They had quite a task, for Jeanne was strong and fought hard, but she could not match two men. They held her, in the end, by the arms, and she was forced to stand still, half way down the steps, and watch.

The children had passed her during her struggle and got to the bottom of the steps. They saw that Raf's guards were released from the handcuffs and one of them was locking them on his wrists again so that his hands were behind his back, as in the chapel that morning.

Julius was standing by his carriage, with his hand on the open door. It was all ready to leave, by the open gates.

A double row of soldiers were taking up their position on the gravel sweep, lining up as a firing party with the front row on one knee. Stenken stood at one end to the side of the line, nearest to Rafael.

Now Raf's guards left him standing alone on the other side of the gravel.

"Oh no, oh no, oh no!" Catherine found she was saying over and over in her anguish.

Julius called out, "Now, run for it, le Marre!"

Raf did not move.

"Shot while trying to escape," the words went through Catherine's mind.

But Rafael was not going to run. He stood still.

Suddenly a small figure ran wildly across the gravel. It was Toby, who had been in the garden and heard the noise. He knew what was happening; he had not escaped across the war-tormented country of north Italy for nothing.

"No, no! Raf!" he shrieked, running across in front of the soldiers and towards Rafael.

"Toby! Go back!" cried Raf, for the soldiers had their rifles raised to fire.

But Toby ran on and flung himself against Raf's legs.

"No, no! Don't! Don't! Don't shoot him!" he screamed, in English.

All three of the other children had instinctively run forward to save Toby, or Raf, or both, they hardly knew.

The soldiers who, although they were Varenshalt's men from Medlerne, were not accustomed to shooting children, lowered their rifles.

Julius shouted to Stenken, who stepped forward and raised his own pistol. He evidently intended to shoot Rafael over the head of Toby. But right in his line of fire was Giles, tall enough to cover Rafael's chest.

"You, boy, move! Get out of the way!" shouted Stenken angrily.

Giles half turned and found himself looking straight into the muzzle of Stenken's pistol, only a few yards away. The face behind it was set hard.

All Giles's instincts told him to jump for it, but something stronger than instinct leapt inside him. He would not, no, he would not move and make it possible for Stenken to shoot down Rafael. Somehow, he hardly knew how, Giles stood without moving for one awful moment, staring back at Stenken.

Then the Civil Guard who looked like Max flung himself at Stenken and brought him, taken by surprise, to the ground.

The execution was delayed, but it could not have been for long, had not somebody come riding through the gates and reined up on the sweep saying, "Hullo, hullo! What sort of a scene is this?"

It was Gabriel d'Altenberg and after him came several armed Nordwick men and Edward on his pony.

Gabriel looked all round; he took in what was happening at once and turned on Julius.

"Now look here, Julius, what the devil are you up to?" he demanded, "Here I come with a letter for you and find you can't wait till midnight to get rid of Rafael le Marre."

"It is not a letter from you I required," said Julius angrily.

"No, but that's what you've got," Gabriel said cheerfully. "Poor Con was in no state to read your treasonable missive. We never gave it to him. Yolande and I thought we would do a little Regencing between us." He turned towards Raf, who was trying to calm Toby, and called out, "I'm sorry, Raf! I ought to have guessed he would not play fair."

"You couldn't have come at a better moment, Gabriel!" answered Raf.

Gabriel laughed. "Julius, you are under arrest for high treason," he said.

But Julius had realized the game was up. He jumped into his carriage and the coachman whipped up the horses. They were out of the gates and down the hill in a few minutes.

"Let's hope he'll be stopped at the frontier," said Gabriel. "I can't spare anyone to chase him till I've got this place cleaned up."

He dismounted and walked over to the soldiers and began to speak to them in the Letzensteiner German. He was wearing only civilian riding dress and though he had a pistol, he had not taken it out. But he behaved as if he was perfectly certain that the Medlerne men would accept his authority and they did. The two who were still gripping Jeanne's arms let go and she immediately went over to Raf and picked up Toby and kissed him. Then, to Giles's surprise, she kissed him too.

"I saw what you did, brave Giles!" she said to him in English.

Giles blushed, but he felt very happy. He saw Raf smiling at him.

"So, now! All is well, Giles, between us?" he said.

Giles nodded; he could not say anything.

Paul said, "Just that minute made all the difference. It gave Max a chance."

"Oh, it *is* Max, is it?" Giles said, glad to divert attention from himself. "I thought it looked like him."

Max, in his borrowed uniform, was still sitting firmly on Colonel Stenken, whom he had long since disarmed. He grinned.

"Good for you, Max!" Raf said, in French. "I wondered when you were going to come into the picture."

"Almost I thought it was going to be impossible, Seigneur," said Max. "In the end they moved so suddenly."

A few minutes later some of the Nordwick men took Stenken in charge and marched him off to the back of the house; he was to be locked up there.

Gabriel came back from the firing party, who were now putting up their weapons.

"It's all right," he said. "They're quite willing to come back under legitimate rule. They obeyed Julius because he's their Duke, but I don't think he's made himself any more popular with them than with our Felsenburgers. Gil said he'd never heard such cheers as when he told them Con was alive."

"And is Con all right?" Raf asked. "We heard he was ill."

"He was ill last Friday, which was just as well for us!" said Gabriel, with a grin. "For you know what old Con is like. If he'd seen that list of signatures Julius sent he'd have felt not wanted and backed out. Really, you know, they were collected while he was thought to be dead. I tell you what, Raf, they were signing up against the idea of twenty years' Regency by me! And I don't blame them!" He laughed aloud. "I daresay you'd have signed too. Well, we had to be tough about you, Raf, and without telling Con. I had to take Yolande to Valmay first. I got here as quickly as I could, but I might have guessed Julius would cheat. As a matter of fact I thought Gilbert would have caught up with him in Felsenbourg. But he's a slippery customer, is Julius."

"You seem to have been pretty slippery yourself,

Gabriel," said Raf. "But you haven't told me about Con. He's not badly ill?"

"No—it was just too much, that night ride on top of everything else," said Gabriel. "He was feverish and light-headed for a bit, that's all. There wasn't time to wait till he'd recovered."

"He's all right now," said Edward d'Altenberg.

"Edward's come from Nordwick today," said Gabriel. "I met him on the bridge just now."

"Con's all right again," said Edward. "And he's coming over here. When he heard about the letter he was very upset and said he couldn't trust Julius—that he'd probably left orders with Colonel Stenken to shoot Raf anyhow, and make it look like an accident."

"Ah," said Raf, "there's one thing Con knows all about, and that's people. He knows Julius, none better."

"So he's coming," said Edward again. "That's why I came first, to see how the land lay. Aunt Genny didn't want me to."

"I bet she didn't!" said Gabriel. "I suppose you just hopped it, as usual. Out of the window? You could have made things much worse, Edward my lad!"

Giles was relieved to hear that Edward too climbed out of windows and acted on ideas his elders thought less bright than he did.

Gabriel was distracted from his nephew by the sight of Rafael swaying on his feet. "Hey, Raf! What's the matter?" he cried, catching hold of him.

"I've just been standing—such a long time," said Raf.

Gabriel held on to him while a soldier was called to unlock the handcuffs and then he took him round the corner of the house and into the sitting room, where the doors, as usual, were standing open to the garden.

Jeanne made Rafael lie down on the couch where they had put Con, though he kept saying he was all right now. Gabriel went into the hall to reorganize the household and later he went down to the village to get the Xandeln men out of gaol.

Max, still in his borrowed Civil Guard uniform, brought wine for Rafael. The children sat round on the floor. Christie ran off to tell the Italians. She had been playing in the garden with Toby when he caught sight of the soldiers lined up to shoot Raf; she had reached the corner just as the little boy ran across the gravel, so she had seen the end of the crisis.

Toby seemed to have recovered from his fright, though he was still white in the face. He insisted on sharing Raf's glass of wine. In between his occasional sips, loudly demanded, he was once more playing with his wooden engine, running it along the mountain ridge of Raf's leg.

"Boom!" he said once, precipitating the engine to catastrophe over an imaginary bridge at Raf's knee.

They were still there, talking, when Con walked through the garden door. Everyone jumped up at the sight of him; even Raf sat up on the couch and the engine suffered another disaster, this time accidental.

Con looked pale and tired but otherwise all right. He sat down on a chair near Raf and scrutinized him. "Well!" he said at last. "I hope you guessed that I wasn't consulted on this Altenberg counter-counter-revolution! My dear Raf, I'm afraid Gabriel ran it very fine. I met him in the village. He never can believe what power does to men who want it, since he couldn't care less about it himself."

"What really finished Julius was Yolande's coup in Valmay," said Rafael. "I can see we've got a Grand Duchess all right, however ready to retire the Grand Duke may be!"

He smiled, and Con smiled back; they understood each other very well.

Now, just at the end of the long grey day, the sun came out under the edge of the cloud and thin yellow light flooded over the country, slanting in at the doors of the garden room.

And next morning the wind was blowing the last wisps of vapour away; the air was bright again, and cooler; there was a feeling that summer was over and autumn coming. The weather had changed.

Constant and Gabriel went to Felsenbourg that day; while they were there the Italians left by train for Belgium and England. Rafael and Jeanne and the children went down to the station to see them off. It was the first time anyone in the village had seen Rafael since he had been held prisoner in his own castle and people kept running out to greet him; they could hardly get through the market place. But there was a train to catch, so they escaped in the end, only to meet another warm welcome from the stationmaster, the ticket clerk and Albert the porter as soon as they reached the station.

Luca Caravelli said, "Raf, my friend, you are king here! Where are your republican ideals?" He laughed. "Your enemies, all the same, seemed more ruthless than mine. This Julius, was he caught at the frontier?"

"No," said Raf. "Who cares? He can't return. If he did, he would be arrested for high treason. Let him live with his wife's relations—a penance for the Austrians, eh?" And they both laughed.

"What about Stenken?" Giles asked. He would never forget Stenken's face behind that gun.

"Court martial for him, I expect," said Raf. "And perhaps rather longer as a prisoner than I was. But Con won't take severe reprisals, you know. He never does, and perhaps he was too lenient with Julius in '48. But now that Julius has shown the full extent of his treason, his exile will be seen to be deserved, and just."

"And will Baron d'Hautrec be exiled too?" Paul asked. He had always thought the diplomatic Baron Rafael's most dangerous enemy.

"Well, it was treason to ask Julius to be Grand Duke," said Raf, "though no doubt he will insist it was the Regency he opposed, as Gabriel said. I suppose he may get back before Julius, but I rather hope he will find Vienna more congenial for retirement than his château over the next hill!"

The train appeared round the bend in the valley. Everyone began saying goodbye, Jeanne kissing Silvia and little Chiara.

When the Italians had climbed on board, Luca leaned out of the window.

"Caterina! Christina! We see you in England? At the British Museum! Raf, you too, please!"

"You want to exhibit me at the British Museum" said Raf. "As what? The last phoenix, poor bedraggled fowl?"

Luca laughed, the train drew off, everybody waved.

To avoid the village they walked round by the river as far as the ferry. The boat had been dredged up and Claus the ferryman was at work cleaning it. He too was delighted to see Rafael again, shaking both his hands and bowing over them.

"Those villains!" he said with feeling. "Those villains! Oh, but Monsieur Rafael, it was fine to see those soldiers stop short when they found there was no ferry across the river and the Grand Duke on the other side! And then to go on to the footbridge and find that blown up by Max! How did you think of it all so quick? Max said, all in a minute."

"Ah, my brain only works fast in emergencies," said Raf. "Needs the stimulus!"

They climbed slowly up the zigzag track from the ferry, which came out at the back of the castle. Going in through the kitchens they did not see that visitors had arrived at the front. So it was quite a surprise to meet Sir Walter and Lady Hawthorne in the hall. They looked as cool and well dressed as ever, but more than a little anxious.

"Giles! Catherine! Are you all right?" Aunt Eleanor said coming over to them at a faster pace than she usually allowed herself, so that her full skirts rustled. "We heard there had been a crisis in Felsenbourg. All sorts of rumours about the Grand Duke. Is he here?"

"Today he is in Felsenbourg, Lady *Autorne*," said Rafael. "But soon he comes back with his wife, to finish their holiday. It was just a bit interrupted."

Lady Hawthorne looked at him suspiciously, the more so because, although he had shaved, his face looked haggard after the strain of the last few days.

"So the children have been alone here with you, Monsieur le Marre," she said. "Why didn't you let us know this change of plan?"

Raf waved his hand. "Somehow there was no opportunity for writing letters," he said, apologetically.

Christie giggled. Lady Hawthorne glanced at her and looked more suspicious than ever. Giles felt he was blushing with embarrassment. He began to say, "You don't understand, Mamma. It's been very . . ."

But Raf put a hand on his arm. "Giles, it's over now. Why alarm your mother? Assure her that all's well that ends well—isn't that right, Miss Lacey? Shakespeare always has the words for the situation!"

Miss Lacey murmured something about its being more like Macbeth or Julius Caesar and Raf began to laugh. He turned to Sir Walter and said, "Come and have a drink, sir, and tell me just what you heard in Brussels about what has been going on in Letzenstein this last week."

But even after this private conversation had taken place Giles did not feel his parents had much idea of what had happened at Xandeln. They heard from Rafael about the bomb attack and that when Julius Varenshalt had proclaimed himself in Felsenbourg the Grand Duke had had to go to Nordwick—and of course they put the best construction on Julius's action, believing his own story (which Rafael gave them) that it was for the sake of his country in a time of crisis. But they seemed to think that during all this excitement Rafael had simply stayed at Xandeln, looking after the children. Giles felt this was not fair, all the more so because of his own part in what had happened. So, in the afternoon, seeing

Raf sitting for once alone in the garden, on one of the benches, he went out to ask him about it.

Raf had the newspaper in his hand but he wasn't reading it; he was just sitting in the sun resting, and rubbing the chin of Miche, Jeanne's Parisian cat, who was rolling lazily on the seat beside him. "Hullo, Giles!" he said.

Giles said, "Why didn't you tell father what really happened here?"

"I thought it better not, Giles," said Rafael. "Somehow it sounds bad that you and Catherine have been living here at the mercy of a man like Stenken. Your parents might refuse to let you visit me again. And I should like you to come many times to Xandeln."

"What, me too?" said Giles, flushing.

"Of course you too, Giles," said Rafael, smiling. "If you had not stood your ground at that critical moment, should I not be dead, or anyway badly wounded, now? I should have tried to jump aside, of course. One can't do that with a firing party but one pistol is worth trying to dodge. But with Toby round my feet and no hands free, it would have been tricky. It was brave of you, Giles, to stand so."

"If you had been shot I would have felt it was my fault," Giles said, and even now he felt dreadful at the thought. "I began to see I was wrong about Julius before we ever got back to Xandeln, because of the way he spoke of the Grand Duke when I told him he was alive. He was very *annoyed* at his being alive."

Raf laughed. "I bet he was! Poor Giles, how were you to know? Julius *looks* all right, unlike some people who are too lazy to shave when life becomes too full!"

Giles felt his face must be redder than ever; he said nothing.

Then Rafael asked, "But why did you think I would do anything against Con? This puzzles me, Giles."

Then Giles had to tell him how Max had said that Rafael himself ought to be Grand Duke, and how this had seemed to confirm what Julius had told him about Raf's rebellious past.

"Oh, good Max!" said Rafael, amused. "He has never been out of Letzenstein, you know—scarcely out of Xandeln. Imagine me a Grand Duke, Giles! I should offend everybody inside of a week—ask your father! No! It needs more patience than I have. It needs a steady reliable person like Con, who takes it as a duty, a service. Julius, no. He must always be imposing his will on others, forcing them to obey. As for me, I am an artist. I draw people as I see them—and that's all I can do for them."

When Giles thought of the three days they had just endured, he felt Rafael had done rather more for people than draw them. He still felt his parents ought to know the truth.

"Well, Miss Lacey will no doubt report on us, Giles," said Rafael. "Let us leave it to her."

"She doesn't know what I did," Giles said.

"So much the better," said Raf. "She will blame it all on Baron d'Hautrec and Colonel Stenken, as bad advisers to Julius. But she will no doubt explain to your parents that I was not in a position to write about what your mother so brilliantly called a change of plan!" He began to laugh again. "Cheer up, Giles! Are we not friends now? I hope so!" He held out his hand and Giles took it, and somehow he felt all right again.

He was really quite glad too not to have to confess to his father that he had been the cause of an incident.

But when Lady Hawthorne commented critically on Rafael's taking the Grand Duke's chair that evening at dinner, it was Giles, not Catherine, who said, "But it is his own chair! Because he is the Seigneur of Xandeln."

And then, of course, Con and Yolande came back and it was once more the Grand Duke who sat at the head of the table.

Con had been ordered to rest by his doctors. He had left the Altenberg brothers in the capital but he brought Edward with him, so that the holiday ended with all the children together again at Xandeln.

And suddenly it was like a holiday again, although a short one, for Sir Walter thought it time to be on the way back to England. It ended with a big picnic by the little river, not far from where the footbridge was being rebuilt. The orphans were included, so it was quite an expedition; a bonfire was lit, sausages frizzled on sticks and potatoes burnt in hot ashes, as well as more palatable cold food distributed from baskets, and a great deal of real lemonade.

"And these lemons, they come from Italy," said Raf. "Like so many good things! May they gain their liberty at last, Luca and his friends."

Raf had brought his guitar slung over his shoulder and after the picnic they all sang songs. Jeanne was teaching the orphans to sing in parts and they were getting quite good at it. Catherine lay on the bank listening, and watching the water slide by; far overhead the great white clouds curled and sailed in a fresh September wind.

It seemed so happy and ordinary, she could hardly believe that only a few days ago they had all been living in a kind of nightmare, expecting the final disaster. As they climbed up the hill towards the castle in the evening she was walking beside Rafael, who was still humming snatches of song, French and German, as he used his stick to help himself up the steep hill.

"The Dragon almost won," she said, half to herself, half to him.

"No, he didn't," said Raf. "He can only win if he turns us into dragons. Killing a few people isn't really a victory for the Dragon, that's the funny thing."

"I don't know about *funny*," said Catherine, with feeling, and Raf laughed.

"No, perhaps I have the wrong word, here," he said. "Funny is like nice, in English; it's used so much one thinks it will do for anything. But really, it's not the Angel who defeats the Dragon, you know. It's the one who was defeated, as I wanted to show in my painting, only the Archbishop didn't understand it."

"Oh, Raf," said Catherine, "what's going to happen about that?"

"I thought I'd paint a vine all over the side walls instead," said Raf. "With faces in the leaves, perhaps. You couldn't pick out the sheep from the goats because they'd be too small. Just as well! Just as it should be! We don't know, do we?"

"But—the end walls?" Catherine was thinking of

the figure of Christ mocked, more than of the Angel and Dragon.

"You know the old canon here?" said Rafael. "He's got interested. He thinks that if we give a great crucifix to hang over the altar, he can persuade the Archbishop to leave St. Michael at the west end, as he is our patron in Letzenstein."

"Is he? I'd forgotten that." Catherine was pleased to remember that this little country, which was her mother's country, had chosen the great Archangel of the heavenly hosts as patron.

"Oh yes, we need a lot of angels to look after us!" said Rafael. "Hundreds of thousands of them! Look at the stars, how many millions there are. Why shouldn't there be as many more beings in the eternal universe who are like stars that know they are stars, like stars that love?" He looked up at the darkening deep blue sky above. "Why not?"

"Raf! Where are you?" Jeanne's voice called from ahead. "Toby has lost his engine!"

"All right!" Raf called back. "I have it in my pocket, Toby. It is travelling by crane. I am the crane!"

Catherine could hear Toby laughing. "Yes, you are like a crane, Raf!" he cried.

They came out of the little wood and there was the castle, with its ruined towers standing up darkly against the fading sky, stars coming out above, owls calling softly, and yellow lights burning in the lower windows of the house.

Rafael leaned on his stick, looking at it. Then he said quietly, "So! We are still here, all of us."

Catherine took his hand and they moved on, last of the trail of people going home. She could hear the river rushing down below, the river that seemed to have carried Con to his death, but he was safe. And the danger of death had gone out of the castle, like the clouds vanishing over the valley.

No one was lost.

About the Author

As children, Meriol Trevor and a friend created highly developed imaginary islands—one for each of them—complete with a rich genealogy of royal families. In writing the *Letzenstein Chronicles,* Miss Trevor has drawn from this treasure trove of characters. The events of this small, fictional country imaginatively reflect the political turmoil of Europe in the late 1840's. She writes: "I decided to use the 'royal' families of Insula as the personal element in the stories— because I believe children find it easier to follow the adventures of persons than political ideas." She continues: "In all my books for children I have concentrated on personal relations, usually with the more serious confrontations between the adults—but also adult/child and child with child —occasioned by the general events going on at the time." The author has a gift of portraying her children *as* children, yet ones who are dramatically involved witnesses to the struggles of their elders.

Born in London in 1919, Miss Trevor graduated from Oxford in 1942. Her first publications were books for children and historical novels. She then wrote a number of acclaimed biographies—including ones on Pope John XXIII, St. Philip Neri and John Henry Newman. In 1967 she was elected a Fellow of the Royal Society of Literature.

Meriol Trevor is the author of many books for children, all of which are pervaded by a gentle wisdom and a love of goodness in ordinary people. *The Letzenstein Chronicles,* written some years ago, are now being published for the first time.

The Letzenstein Chronicles
by Meriol Trevor

The Crystal Snowstorm (Book 1)

It is the eve of 1848, a time of small revolutions throughout Europe. Young Catherine Ayre has been called from her quiet home in England by a grandfather she scarcely knows, Grand Duke Edmond of Letzenstein. She becomes a pawn in the political unrest of the small country. Why does her grandfather so hate her uncle Constant, the rightful heir? And just who is Rafael le Marre? Catherine is swept into a number of exciting adventures before she is able to answer these questions and feel herself a part of the small but fascinating country of Letzenstein.

Following the Phoenix (Book 2)

It is February, 1848. Paris is in Revolution. Unconventional Rafael le Marre has become guardian of Paul Cardomel, a 14-year-old English boy. They must secretly leave the city. Assisting in Raf's plan of escape is the independent-minded Jeanne, a dancer, and Christie, the daughter of an English railroad magnate. It should all have gone smoothly, had not Raf run afoul of his old, jealous political enemies of Letzenstein. Paul, Christie, Jeanne —and Rafael above all—face anguished moments until hope at last wins its reward.

The Rose and Crown (Book 4)

Melisande, a London girl with booksellers' and actors' blood in her veins, often finds life dreary; her family struggles to run a carters' inn, "The Rose and Crown." Then, in November 1849, Rafael le Marre of Letzenstein arrives, bringing Mel's lost cousin Toby with him. New friends and unexpected experiences swirl in Rafael's wake: among others, Melisande meets Catherine Ayre; and Charley the sweeper adds cockney mischief. Raf stirs up the trouble that is native to his frank character in whatever land he is in. But in this case it is Toby who creates the most breathless moments. Several necessary resolutions must occur before Raf and company may set out once again for beloved Letzenstein.